I0541447

The Bad News
Cafe

Hunter S. Fatback

The Bad News Cafe

ISBN: 978-0-9991497-0-6
ISBN-13: 978-0999149706 (Charasma)

For my friend Judy- you were supposed to be here to
remind me not to quit my day job

The Bad News Cafe

INTRODUCTION

I honestly don't give a fuck what you put on your hot dog. For me, anything more than two toppings is too much. I prefer mustard when it comes to solo condiments, but if you like ketchup there's no reason to be ashamed. I don't recall exactly when hot dogs and their correct toppings became a unit of measure for the gastronomically adept. My mind goes back to trace the timeline and I remember a simpler era. I remember before food programming hit a point of saturation where a well-produced and informative show like "The Mind of a Chef" would be considered the Masterpiece Theatre of the foodie kingdom. It really wasn't that long ago when you think about it. The high point of any foodie evening used to be when Emeril Lagasse would pull the knobs right off of his stove, hold them up to the camera and tell you…*those knobs are there for a reason!* And also nobody likes one sided tasting food, so season both sides! I should have seen the writing on the wall the first time I wanted to tell someone, "Hey, screaming BAM is totally played out now." Because Emeril's show was on four times every damn night. And it goes back farther than that. I'm not old enough to remember watching "The Galloping Gourmet," but I definitely remember sitting at my grandparents' house watching "Graham Kerr's Kitchen" on PBS. He'd end the show with a little whiteboard presentation of the health values of his meal. I'd wonder, "What is *this* shit? Is there a Julia Child rerun coming on soon? Please?" I can't remember all of the shows we watched, but Martin Yan, Justin Wilson, Nathalie Dupree, Jacques Pepin and Jeff Smith were in heavy rotation. I also remember the day that Channel 2 in Kansas City suddenly became MTV. For the first year or so I think they just played the same Rod Stewart videos, but by the time we were enjoying pre-scandal Frugal Gourmet episodes, MTV had already started to lose its focus on music. When my favorite show "Dining Around" was pulled from the lineup on the fledgling Food Network, I should have known that the same shift was imminent. The network jumped the shark when they gave Mario Batali a goofy sidekick to accompany him to Italy. Oh, the antics that followed…they may as well have named him Cousin Oliver. Then the homey façade took the biggest hit when Alton Brown got enough post-Good Eats, pre-Cutthroat Kitchen camera time to reveal that he is indeed the dourest Episcopalian grandmother in all the land. But now "Good Eats" is coming back? I don't know, I guess learning the four-hour and/or overnight method to make your grilled cheese will be thrilling for someone. And honestly, the channel has gotten so bad that even people who can't stand Alton Brown must be looking at it like the prospect of Mitt Romney in 2017 vs. the 2012 Romney. Maybe he won't be so bad now if you consider the current state of affairs.

Anyway, that hot dog. Somehow it became patient zero in this media-driven culture. Attention spans are shot to hell. We used to just have Chowhound, a few decent blogs, and print media was not quite breathing its last. Now all of that spare time is parsed, pulverized and dispersed via gigantic digital networks of opinions, trends, pretty pictures and predictions. The humble hot dog and the single correct way to eat it if you're older than five became the tip of the spear. In the cyclone of information overload, it is the anchor, the primary key for everyone to share. On this very evening, relationships will be strengthened or destroyed over ketchup. Because wherever you are in America when that sun goes down and the evening star shines bright on your piece of this great land, you don't have to have much money or available dining options to know mustard is what separates you from the boundless legions of the blissfully ignorant.

This story may be painfully Midwestern to some. That is probably just my culinary inferiority complex speaking. The Midwest is where I grew up and it is where I currently reside. Barring an incredible job offer or sudden fame as a blogger whose writing has more than ten followers, this is where I plan to stay. With friends in almost all states and across parts of the globe (thanks to the same technology that has decimated our attention spans), everybody's upbringing and culinary experiences wind up sounding more interesting than mine. Growing up in a poor neighborhood in Kansas City, Kansas, we ate most of our meals at home. I think I was around ten when we got our first McDonald's a couple of miles from our house, and that was a big damn deal. Going out to eat was either burgers at one of the many local drive-ins, or it was Sunday dinners someplace like The Forum Cafeteria at Indian Springs Mall, Mexican food at La Cocina or Italian food at Jenny's. Sometimes our entire extended family would get together on the weekend for a fried chicken feast at a place called Mrs. Peters. There were countless picnics and potlucks, and shopping at farmer's markets and roadside stands for our fresh fruits and vegetables was just a normal part of life. The retelling of my first experience at a Chinese restaurant in my early teens was equal to or greater than Jack London's *The Call of the Wild* among my peers. In hindsight, I think it was all pretty awesome. Hipster kitsch thirty-five years or so ahead of its time. I'm sure trends existed, but there was no easy digital transfer of information from the coasts. Everything was word-of-mouth, and dining wasn't an achievement. Today everything with a dollar value associated with it is assigned a noun and verb: trend and trending. A big flash-forward from the smell of sterno heating the chicken skewers on my very first Pu-Pu Platter all the way to current day. Kansas City officially has trends. We have access to enough options to judge the best and the worst of whatever is trending. Does your town have ramen? After a whole lot of talk and anticipation we finally got ramen. And now we even have enough ramen to rate it by completely arbitrary standards and never, ever flinch in the face of a differing opinion. Our dumpling game isn't very strong, though. And we don't have a good enough representation of regional Thai to speak intelligently about it beyond our borders. I picked those three things because they tend to appear regularly on the Eater, Munchies, and Lucky Peach (before it became *The New Yorker* and then set a retirement date) sites. Those have been three of the main industry barometers for people who want to sound like an authority without going anywhere. So we've got trends and we're getting more and more press. I think that's fantastic, but there is one unique aspect of the metro area I should bring up for anyone reading or writing about our restaurants. Kansas City, Kansas, and Kansas City, Missouri, are two completely different cities in two completely different states. I can't remember which magazine it was, but one of our nationally-recognized restaurants on the Missouri side got a nod as one of the "Best Restaurants in Kansas." Granted, it can get confusing because you can literally drive on State Line Road and see one town on your left and the other on your right. If you don't know whether you're heading north or south, an easy way to tell them apart is that a gallon of gas costs around seven cents more on the Kansas side of the street. I fucking love my towns and the people who live here…I grew up in Kansas City, Kansas, but have lived on the Missouri side for most of my adult life. I will admit that I get a little protective. I have a tendency to react strongly at times. We're still just flyover country to many, so we're vulnerable to that one customer who gained a lifetime of ramen wisdom and knowledge during that single five-day trip to Japan. Our job market has gotten strong enough to draw folks from larger food towns like Chicago. Let me tell you, it takes good timing to squeeze in a word when some of them start name-dropping far superior restaurants to wherever it is you just mentioned to them. They have to breathe, so that's your best bet to wedge a syllable in there. That's just the way it goes. A chef can spend their entire career perfecting their pasta techniques, but on any given evening when that plate hits the table, their credibility depends upon how closely they mirror that one dinner during a single visit to Rome when that person had something similar. But much better. Because, well, it was Rome.

I tended bar for a while more than twenty years ago, but other than that I have had no professional role in the service industry. The local character I play is that of the recovering alcoholic who will always manage to worm that into the conversation, and will always have to have an unhealthy, obsessive relationship with something that doesn't kill as quickly as booze or drugs. I seek the approval of my friends by writing shit like this, but I mainly show up at the same places to eat or hang out over and over. I'm just an observer, and from time to time will rely upon the ubiquitous food blog to offer my unique perspective on dining in my town.

The thing that started me down the path to writing this story was an offer from the editor of an online magazine to cover a restaurant that had gotten on the radar of a handful of industry folks. The short version of the story: I was happy for the opportunity and had every intention of delivering. But it quickly got way bigger than anything I could fit into a 4,000-word article. So this is me doing my best to tell a story worthy of the restaurant and its staff.

As far as hands-on industry work goes, I will be the first to admit I do not have the temperament for it. The restaurant industry is a place where any random customer has the power to go online and rebrand their ego as community service. Or they can rely on bottom of the barrel socialization to band together with like-minded socially inept enthusiasts in order to create the illusion of influence. Yelp is the easiest example, along with a minefield of "expert" social media groups. Granted, I'm an asshole with tunnel vision whenever I get something that annoys me in my crosshairs, but I've never met an Elite Yelper (that is a real thing) who was any more interesting or insightful than a cardboard cutout of themselves would be. If I ever get to the point where my idea of a community is a group of people who pride themselves on doing the highest number of painfully subjective reviews in a year, I hope someone has the humanity to lay down a plastic tarp for the mess and then put one in the back of my head. The next step in their assimilation is being familiar enough with all of the bullshit metrics Yelp uses to justify their enabling of clueless assholes, to quote them like scripture. And honestly, when the only reviews from *The New York Times* that get on anyone's radar are basically just hit pieces on the lowest and highest echelon restaurants, how do you expect people with little knowledge and even less discipline to act? Hospitality means you can never just tell someone to shut up and stop being a fucking idiot, and in a real-time digital world that is incredibly empowering to idiots. And apparently, hospitality also means having a constant story arc to keep people reading every single Top 25 list and a flood of details about anticipated restaurant openings. And of course restaurant closings where everyone gets to weigh in about the root cause and how they saw it coming the whoooole time. I would simply like to sit back and enjoy where we are for a little longer before we get hit with random proclamations from food media, like — the death of fine dining is here! Or, the entire restaurant industry is a bubble that is about to *burst*! Seriously, our guy just got the Beard award for best chef in the Midwest a couple years back. Can we let fine dining live for a little while longer? Because that's what he does. We'd all appreciate it very much if the entire industry didn't implode. His foie gras torchon is possibly the best in the world. Do we need that level of drama to give people something to talk about? Is our attention deficit disorder so bad that we have to turn something we do every single day of our lives anyway into an achievement based on an unrealistic level of importance? Sometimes I feel like we have taken the most primal, basic instinct to a point that dwarfs the mapping of the human genome. I wonder if it's the food that truly matters or if the same people would find some other thing to overthink if Food Network never happened.

Part of it is trying to justify my fancy psychology book learning and part is my naturally creepy voyeuristic nature, but I have watched the digital culture split into two groups of people who are the best at eating. One group has a *lot* of money, and the other has *no* money. If you have a lot of money, people can know you're good at eating because of the pictures from all of the $100 minimum entry per person dinners and events you attend. Kansas City has way more of those than you'd think. If you have no money, that is great too because you bring an everyman voice to this dialogue that consists of pictures of a lot of food trucks, holes in the wall and random ethnic spots nobody has heard of in parts of town where nobody wants to go. You have to be careful though because the people *with* money enhance their profile by journeying to a ghetto once every few weeks for a meal. If you truly love a place, it's best to sacrifice the associated street cred and never mention it. Kansas City is sort of a small town with big media aspirations, so when you do find a local gem you hit it hard because as soon as one blog, website or magazine gets wind of it, the race is on for all of them to cover the exact same story in the exact same way. Restaurant openings and closings, new chefs at old restaurants, old chefs at new restaurants, every event, every trend that finally made its way in from the coasts...all are covered nearly identically in the usual places within days if not hours of each other. Planting your flag on a story *first* has become more important than the quality or the content of the story itself. A new restaurant can be old news before the fucking dessert course is served during the soft opening. It will live out its media lifecycle via random foodie blogs, the major indie periodicals, local paper, locally hosted radio shows, and sometimes television. Staying power will depend upon repeat business that comes from the quality of their product and service, along with some luck. It's a fickle and unpredictable business. The scary final stop before being relegated to the lost and forgotten media boneyard involves painfully staged photos of one of the aforementioned people with a *lot* of money mugging for the camera and pretending to take a bite of something; the overly-processed picture posted on Instagram, but it was taken on a full frame DSLR and has a watermark. So that counts as media.

I am trying not to veer too far into ranting asshole blogger territory, which if I'm being completely honest, has been my milieu. I will admit that I was pretty excited when someone in "the food media" reached out to me and asked me to do an article for them. When you don't actually work in the industry, and people you don't know start to recognize you or reach out to you for different things, it's a little flattering but mostly awkward.

Doing an article on a restaurant in Topeka seemed simple enough at first, but I am like a deer in the headlights if I have a deadline and someone is going to be editing whatever I write. Plus, I'm the Kansas City guy. I own this town. I'm not the Topeka guy. The restaurant in question was supposedly a place where all of the customers had suffered some kind of loss, heartbreak or tragedy...their meal was a pilgrimage of sorts.

Nobody I knew had investigated the origin of the story or how accurate it was, but the restaurant was a physical place and the writer reached out to me because of the owner's connection to Kansas City, Kansas. It's not nearly as big as Kansas City, Missouri, but I thought it was an awfully big assumption on their part to think I'd know this particular guy. Well, it ended up that I did indeed know this particular guy. At least peripherally.

Joe Juric, the chef and owner, and I went to the same grade school and early junior high, and we had a lot of the same friends, but we weren't running buddies. We had some bad characters in common, but he moved away before anyone was going to jail or dying or anything. I was into a lot of different stuff, but managed to stay out of real trouble. For example, I didn't steal cars, but would get phone calls on random Saturday mornings from people asking if I knew who *did* steal their car.

One friend we had in common was someone I saw relatively regularly. Our friend Steven and I were in school together all the way through high school graduation. I had no idea if they stayed in touch after high school, but you rarely saw one of them without the other at parties or concerts even after Joe moved to Topeka. I'm someone who relies upon inside connections and first person reports exclusively…I would skip writing the story altogether if it meant I had to cold call the restaurant.

My potential inside guy Steven was always a good kid in school. He was the type who would never get involved in any real criminal activity, but he could be shamed into being a lookout. And he wouldn't rat anyone out. He was taller than the rest of us, rail thin and had a white guy afro…think of a dishwater blonde Bob Ross, but malnourished. So as partners in crime go, he would be in far more danger than the rest of us if someone had to pick him out of a lineup. We graduated before "The Simpsons" was on TV, but if we hadn't his nickname would have been Sideshow Bob…no question.

Steven worked in the Crossroads Arts District near downtown KC in a similar field of IT as myself. I ran into him pretty often considering the amount of time I spend down there. I reached out to him and we had a late lunch one afternoon so that we could catch up and I could find out what he knew about Joe's place. Unfortunately, Steven's amazing hair was a victim of time, but other than that he was the same old skinny kid from Wyandotte County. We chatted about the food scene and I found out what little he knew about our friend Joe's restaurant. They had stayed in touch off and on over the years, but Steven had never been out to eat at the restaurant. I thought it would add a level of vetting if I had him reach out to Joe first, so I gave him my number to pass along with the plan being to make a trip to Topeka in the near future.

My amateur analysis of the absurdity and

necessity of modern food culture started sometime last year, but was exacerbated by the overall shittiness of 2016. As the year finally released us from its grasp, I wanted to try and come to terms with the sweeping changes and the people we lost. Any excitement over getting some experience with professional food writing was squashed by the questionable future of my company's contract with our current client, which we learned about at the first of the year. So my quest to rethink my priorities within the local food community had a sudden jolt of reality that overshadowed my self-absorbed existential musings. Any pressure I was feeling to get more of my favorite spots into regular rotation could be removed via sudden loss of any disposable income. But some of the same questions remained, no matter the motivation.

When is food more than just food? Where does being a regular in a restaurant stop and real friendship begin? Shortly after I got sober I began to wonder how to make sense of dining now that my usual bourbon and wine rituals were no longer part of it. Those accounted for much more than I wanted to admit. For me the new way of approaching everything was to make it about the people. If I knew one farmer or one chef, through the natural course of our relationship I'd learn about other farmers, producers and chefs that they appreciated. Word-of-mouth ended up becoming the way that I relearned my city. I like to think that you'd hear me talk as much about the people as the food anyplace where I'm a regular. All of that is a critical part of sense memory for me.

I started digging back into my mind to trace people and meals all the way back into my childhood. There were of course all of the birthdays and holidays, but they all eventually ran together. I suddenly recalled for the first time in years how after the first time I ever saw someone get shot we went to Kokomo Drive-In on Leavenworth Road. The food was never as good as Peter's Drive-In on State Avenue, but in those moments of complete shock and sensory overload you stick with what's low-key. And all of those first dates at Metropolis, with women I would never get to sleep with even though I was fancy enough to take them someplace where fried oysters were in the salad and one sauce even had caviar. Awkward moments either highlighted or soothed by food. Job stress, pressure to use proper grammar for the first time since grad school, doubts about how my philosophical priorities were playing out in the real world...all of those indulgent white people problems were bubbling in my brain when I finally got in my car to head to Topeka. Unsure about my footing in the world, there was something strangely comforting about visiting a restaurant where people supposedly went after someone died, or was dying, going through a divorce, needed to declare they wanted a divorce, got bad news from the doctor, or whatever else. Those were all things Steven mentioned from his limited knowledge of the restaurant's protocol. What did they eat that was so special and why was my old friend Joe the person who cooked it for them? At a difficult time in your life, whatever it was, it was the place you went. So I headed out.

-1-

I'd heard about the restaurant The Five in passing, but didn't know that it used to be Juric's. I would always pass by Juric's on Topeka Boulevard whenever I was finding my way over to Porubsky's to get those hellish hot pickles. Porubsky's is in the "Little Russia" neighborhood of Topeka. It's a tiny family-owned grocery store, deli, tavern and restaurant all in one, and a mandatory stop anytime I'm in the area. They have excellent chili, but the hot pickles are their claim to fame. I don't think I ever actually ate them. I'd let them sit in the refrigerator waiting for them to mellow out a little bit, but what always happened was I'd forget about them until I couldn't trust if they were still okay to eat or not. I never ate at Juric's even though the dining choices were slim on that side of Topeka. It was obviously a mom-and-pop type of place, but if you're from the Midwest you understand that the majority of those restaurants are for hardcore regulars and travelers who think the food is automatically going to be great. That is usually not the case. I'm not always the quickest at putting things together. Knowing that Juric's existed and that a chef named Joe Juric ran The Five which was also on Topeka Boulevard finally made it click that it was the same location. Steven confirmed it was the same building, same family, but it went through major changes over the past few years.

Originally owned by Joe's parents, they operated Juric's for nearly twenty-five years after relocating to Topeka. It was a family-style lunch and dinner spot that served soups, stews and sandwiches, along with full dinners in the evening. With what I could find out about it online and from Steven, they did great Reubens and patty melts, as well as a famously massive Chef's Salad with or without the nuclear Porubsky hot pickles on the side. Huge portions in the Midwest are key to having what sounded like a large, local following. Dinner specials featured meatloaf, roasted chicken, liver and onions, and sausage and sauerkraut that were both made by Joe's dad. He also cured the briskets they used for their Reubens and corned beef and cabbage entrée. His mom made all of the homemade desserts, meaning she made them at their house and drove them the short distance to the restaurant. Selections changed daily, often more than once per day if something sold out and there was time to make more.

Mrs. Juric passed away in 2009, which left her husband and Joe's older brother Tom to run the family business. The restaurant originally opened in 1990 and Tom Juric began working there with his parents after getting out of the Army and moving back home in 1995. His official role was that of general manager, which meant everything from ordering, prepping and cooking to serving and cleaning. Joe had some experience working at the restaurant sporadically through the years, but his primary occupation was managing a local print shop until 2012. Early that year, the brothers lost their dad and Joe quit his job to focus on the family business full time. Shortly after that, the restaurant was rebranded as The Five. I found no additional information about the name change at first. I thought maybe the brothers were major fans of the Fox News program or something. With it being Topeka, that would draw customers. The other major changes were the first-ever alcohol sales, and the switch to dinner service only. Overall, the story of The Five read like dozens of other restaurants that have come and gone over the years. Popular mom and pop establishments will have a long run in the community before some circumstance shifts ownership and management to family members or longtime employees. There is usually some degree of rebranding that more often than not has a brief lifespan before the business closes. The story I was tasked to dig into, which was confirmed by Steven, was specific…it was much more than a change in theme or brand; The Five was the death and bad news restaurant. Of course, I wanted to know more.

It was a couple of weeks later, but I did hear from Joe and he sounded more than happy to have me come out to the restaurant for a chat. The way he put it, he hadn't had anyone outside his clientele ask about "the bad news café" in at least a year. While discussing specifics, he told me I was welcome to come up as early as 10:30 or 11:00am on a Tuesday or Wednesday if I didn't mind hanging out while they got the place ready for service. I am not great at interviewing people, so the last thing I wanted to do was show up with no point of reference beyond Steven's brief history lesson and internet scraps if I was going to spend the day. There was no social media presence for The Five, but searches on everyone's name and the name of the restaurant did yield new information, including one tragic detail. Tom Juric died suddenly in December of 2014, leaving behind one ex-wife, two step-children, and his younger brother Joe. That was all the obituary on the *Topeka Capital-Journal* website reported. The archives did also mention The Five by name in two different articles. One was a brief crime report stating that an off-duty Shawnee County Sheriff's deputy was arrested for assault inside The Five in July of 2015. The other was a full article published about a month later that contained the most details about the restaurant I was ever going to find before I met with Joe. The focus was on Joe, his family's history in the Topeka restaurant community, the loss of his family members, and his decision to continue as executive chef and general manager of The Five. The nugget was finding the origin of the name.

"The Five" was the name chosen by the brothers to honor their father Daniel Juric and his four closest friends. The five men served together in Vietnam, and over the years all had taken residence in Topeka for various reasons, chief of which was the bond formed in surviving the war. Daniel was the first of the men to pass away, and the article included some nice thoughts and memories from his friends. That was the entirety of what I knew about Juric's and The Five before I got in my car to go meet Joe on an unseasonably warm Tuesday morning in late January.

Topeka is not generally a destination for me. There is the state capital, a great history museum, and for a long time it had one of the last A&W drive-in restaurants in the region. Not one of the new Long John Silver's/A&W hybrids, an actual sit-down restaurant and drive-in complete with the frosty mugs. It's a nice town. One unfortunate claim to fame is the Westboro Baptist compound. Whether or not someone knows the church by name, they have absolutely heard of the "God Hates Fags" people. When they aren't being ambassadors for the angry Old Testament God by picketing funerals and anyplace else where their attention whoring will get them on television, those bundles of sunshine are a mere hour or so down the road from Kansas City. Other than the occasional stop at Porubsky's, northwest Topeka remained a mystery to me. North of I-70 and the Kansas River, it is a bit like a small town within a slightly larger town. The Five is situated off the main drag east of Northwest Topeka Boulevard, not far from Morse Street. If you want to purchase a used car, have one worked on while getting your hair and nails done, or require more than one convenience store in a two-block radius, you can't beat the neighborhood.

The Five itself is not an inviting building. Word of mouth and repeat business was obviously key to its successful run as Juric's, but I was curious to learn more about what drew people there now. Joe mentioned on the phone that in addition to the hours change, the menu had been completely revamped from family-style a la carte to a three-course prix fixe format. Whether or not the urban legend was true, it sounded like a restaurant worth checking out and I'd have the opportunity to catch up with an old friend.

Approaching the restaurant from the east, a large gravel parking lot surrounded by a waist-high retaining wall makes it look a little like a funeral home. The wide cement patio between the lot and the building, abandoned except for one picnic table on the north end, could have easily served as a car port where a hearse was loaded once upon a time. It was probably too small to ever be a funeral home, but there's no way it was always a restaurant...a pawn shop, porn store, tax office or shady chiropractor maybe, but not a restaurant. I arrived a little after 10:30am and saw no signs of life other than an occasional passing car as I looked around outside and took a few notes. Looking up and down the street, it was the only block I could see in the immediate area where the sidewalks had not completely broken down and given way to grass and weeds. The cinderblock building is painted tan with two stacked concrete slabs that function as steps leading to a narrow red brick entryway with a shingled arch roof. A single light fixture is attached to the front of the arch, pointed straight down to light the steps. At night, it surely achieves maximum effect on the brushed silver lettering just below it that spells out "The Five." Three street lights in the parking lot and that one bulb are the only things in the immediate area that would provide visibility in the evening. Two large windows were on either side of the doorway once upon a time, but only the frames remain now. They are filled in with wood panels and painted the same color as the rest of the building. On the east side of The Five there are a few small windows, but they are positioned too high for anyone to see in or out of, and are covered by sets of security bars. It was a safe assumption that the natural lighting inside could only rival that of the Jackson County jail. I stepped past the winter curtains hanging in front of the outer entryway to see if there was a window in the door to get a look inside. Just as I started to peer through the door, a partially obscured face stared at me as it opened halfway.

"Hey buddy!"

My first reaction when Joe popped his head around the door was to feel old. I hadn't seen him since we were kids, and there we were meeting again in the upper end of our forties. It was funny to see him look like one of the "old" men from our neighborhoods. Historically there was always a sizeable Slavic population in Kansas City, Kansas. Most people used and still use the term Croatian for everyone who grew up in a neighborhood called

Strawberry Hill, but that is probably because they've never referred to a Serbian as a Croatian to their face. Or vice versa. In my limited non-Catholic, German-Hispanic experience, the majority of my friends were Croatian but you tried to never assume. I couldn't remember Joe's story, maybe Serbian with his dark wavy hair, but everything else was just like the old neighborhood.... medium height, arms corded with muscle, and a respectable beer belly. The weird thing about those beer bellies, and this is usually learned too late in the middle of a drunken altercation, is that they are absolutely rock hard. Bizarre, but true. Anyway, there weren't any notable points of reference between us other than our friend Steven, so I led with that.

"Chef! Thanks for this! I'm glad Steven told me to come out and check out what you're doing."

"Welcome! Welcome, come on in…come in!" he said, leading me through the doorway. "So what's the word on the street? You come here when you flunk algebra or your grandma died or something?"

"Something like that," I chuckled, "I'll be honest, I don't know much at all besides what I could find in the paper."

"Ha, pissed off cops and war heroes…" he paused

31

for second. Then he looked at me and said, "I hope the truth isn't too boring compared to whatever you've heard. I should have had you here yesterday! Deep cleaning day. Could have gotten work out of you. Scrubbing and dusting. Anyway, come check the place out."

The morning sun made the inside of The Five seem darker than it already was. When my eyes adjusted and I looked around the room, it had more of a homey feel to it than I expected from the outside. The dated décor makes it relaxed and comforting. Immediately inside the front door is a bar on the right, with six or eight stools and a banquette with three small tables lining a wall that separates the bar from the main dining room. At the end of the banquette closest to the front door is a small host station. The floors are well-worn hardwoods, and the walls are a light tan throughout. On the other side of the wall from the bar is another banquette that stretches from the doorway to the far end of the dining room next to the kitchen entrance. Photos and paintings hang on the walls. Mostly family photos, vintage city and farm scenes. What had to be pictures of Joe's parents and his brother were prominently displayed on both sides of the kitchen entrance. Most interesting are two display cases inside the old window frames that are boarded from the outside. The various pictures, tchotchkes, trophies, dolls and books sit behind glass and possess obvious significance for the Juric family. A five-dollar bill looked like it had been laminated to the wall right above and between the cases. No autographs or well wishes were written on it, which is often the case for a restaurant's first official transaction. I didn't want to ask about it, but I knew there had to be a story since it was placed above the cases of family heirlooms. In addition to the small amount of light coming in from the windows on the west wall, the room is illuminated by plain globe fixtures hanging from the ceiling. At full capacity, the bar would hold around a dozen people. Simple bistro style tables and chairs are situated in the dining room in a configuration that has two tops along the banquette and west wall, and four tops down the middle of the room. The whole room would be easy to reconfigure for smaller or larger parties, but by my count it could seat forty to fifty people.

"The bar is new," Joe said. "I mean, it's new to The Five. It used to be one big room, but when we shut the place down for a few months after our dad died, we put in the bar, the wall, the bench seating."

"It looks good," I told him, "It looks like it's always been here. It's a place I'd go. Booze is a new thing here?"

"Yeah, oh yeah. Never would have happened with my parents. Not because they didn't drink though," he explained. "They weren't huge drinkers, but this town had blue laws for a long time and it wasn't worth the hassle to go for a liquor license in a family restaurant. What we're doing now though, liquor is a no-brainer. No shit, we sell a lot."

"I can imagine!" I laughed.

"Hey Jerry! Speaking of Stevie, he told me you were like Mr. French!"

That caught me off-guard. "Who? Like the butler from *Family Affair*?"

"No! Oh shit that would be funny though. No, the guy from *The Departed*. You see that? The guy who was Nicholson's right hand."

"Yeah, yeah, yeah...Ray Winstone. I like him a lot. You see him in *Sexy Beast*?"

"No, never heard of it." He answered.

"Well," I told him, "you have to check that one out. I can't not watch the whole thing when it comes on

34

TV. Steven though, that's funny. I think I know what he's talking about, but I've had pretty much straight jobs for twenty years now." I assumed he was referring to a stretch of time from my mid-20's to early 30's where I leave big gaps in my personal history. I didn't remember talking to Steven about any of that, it comes up once per year at the most, but we had a lot more people than Joe in common over the years. "There was a period when I was sort of a Dear Abby for some sociopathic types, but I was never shooting people in the knee to show off to Leonardo DiCaprio...."

"Ha ha ha! Oh shit, who knows where Stevie got that from. So you married and all that?" he asked.

"Yeah, wife and kid, suburban life. I can still see Wyandotte County from my house though."

"Wyco...I go there for food from time to time, but damn it has been a while." He motioned me over to the bar and we both took a seat. "So shit has to get done today, but I had both of my cooks come in early to free me up. Usually one comes in around nine with the morning dishwasher, but I had them both come in for morning and afternoon prep. My sous can decide if and when to cut someone loose tonight. I'll have to get some things done here and there, and jump in for service." Then he added, "I appreciate you offering to help with prep, but I can't yell at you for doing something wrong and I guarantee you would do something wrong. What time you have to leave?"

"I'm here however long is okay," I explained, "there's no set agenda. I'll record our talks if that's all right, but it's up to you what's on and off the record. I'm just interested in what your restaurant is about...filling in some blanks." I showed him my digital recorder and turned it on. I wanted to get as much information as I could without coming across like an over-anxious reporter. In my limited experience, the conversation needs to flow as naturally as possible. I'd be there all day so I planned to let him set the pace.

"Oh, okay. Recording is cool and I'm not going to incriminate myself, so do whatever you want. Like I told you on the phone, this is the first time I've been approached for anything like this, so with it being an old neighborhood guy asking, the timing feels right. I like what we have here. I'm proud of what we've got. It has been fucking weird thinking how I'm supposed to explain it, but I put some thought into how to approach it. If you need any specifics just let me know."

"The goal is to get enough material to submit for an online magazine in Kansas City. Beyond that, I just want to know about the restaurant operations, you and your family, where the new reputation came from, whatever you're comfortable with," I told him. "It was weird timing to hear about your restaurant towards the end of a bad year. This sounds like a good focal point for me right now..."

Joe interrupted, "You want something? Stevie mentioned you don't drink, but we've got a whole bar! I'm going to have a beer."

"Water is great, thanks."

He walked behind the bar to get a glass and crack open a beer, and began chuckling to himself. "Yeah, been a *few* bad years here, decade actually...but no social media, I don't do any of that. Not for the restaurant anyway. The most we did was a Value Mail flyer before we re-opened as The Five, but got nothing from that. We don't have a website at all, just no time for it, but I had some fucking guy from Yelp call me a couple of months ago wanting me to buy ads or something. Really annoying. What's your take on Yelp?" he asked. His eyebrows were raised in a way that let me know even if I didn't already dislike Yelp I'd get points for hammering it.

I told him, "It's a good place to find an address or look at a menu, but Yelpers take themselves too seriously. I don't have a single good friend in the industry who views it positively, but you have to play the game or they get their feelings hurt…it's extortion basically." Joe was nodding his head so I continued. "I look at it like the most socially ill-equipped people who don't really understand the business, weaponizing their influence so they can pretend they are players in the industry. But they are not. They don't know shit. There are just a lot of them and Yelp incentivizes constant reviews. If you put together an event for them and give them stuff for free, they spread the word about your business."

Joe kept nodding in agreement and said, "I don't know a lot about it, but I trust other chefs and friends from here in Topeka, and it's more bullshit than benefit. It takes me three minutes of reading to get pissed. I think you nailed it. People who don't know a fucking thing about this business beyond the two hours their ass is in a seat. And they don't have to. They don't have shit to lose. They're too stupid to know how they can fuck a small business over an issue that doesn't mean anything. I've had foodies hear about the place and make a production about coming in. They're annoying but I haven't seen us pop up on Yelp, good or bad."

Joe's speech and mannerisms went back and forth between his hands and mouth fighting for equal time in a rapid retelling of a story, to slowing way down as he eased deeper into contemplation, rubbing his forehead as he searched for the best way to state his thoughts. His eyes were either pointed right at mine or searching someplace just beyond the crown molding above the bar mirror. He was deliberate in his speech and obviously didn't want to leave out a significant thought or detail, but he also didn't waste time or stray very far from a point. I began to relax, the worst-case scenario for the day would be good conversation. Joe was finishing his beer and explaining how he only carried bottled beer even though kegs were cheaper, because fuck cleaning taps. And how his bar manager took him at his word that he would never buy a blender. They had a wide selection of liquor, but no drink menu. Instead of risking the time it would take to get his thoughts on mixology, I took a chance and asked, "So how about the cop who got arrested?"

"Oooh, we'll get to that. We will definitely get to that. Sorry, I just didn't expect to enjoy having my guys downstairs doing everything this much. It's nice to sit in my own place."

I felt like I had knocked him off balance. "Sorry, no rush, it's your story."

He rested his elbows on the bar, turned his head to me and said, "If you're here for the day you'll see and hear as much as we can fit in. People either live here and know me and my restaurant or there's what you found in the paper. And that's it. So I guess to start off I'll say that idiot Fox News show had nothing to do with The Five, and people do ask about that...but neither did a group of old Vietnam veterans." He suddenly sat up straight, smiled and said, "I figure the best place to start is with my menu! You want to check out my menu?"

"I'd love to see your menu, Chef."

-2-

Joe grabbed another beer from the bar and walked over to the host station to pick up a couple of their one-page menus. Then he motioned for me to follow him and we walked through the dining room, stopping at the last four top closest to the kitchen. From there I could hear male voices from time to time, sometimes muffled and coming from downstairs, other times louder as they worked in the kitchen. There was a minute or so when I heard someone yell something in Spanish, and then switch to English and berate what I assumed was another cook, "What did I say? What did I say? You fucked it up! No! Fix that shit!" I couldn't make out the reply, but it was over quickly. I smelled some kind of meat cooking shortly after walking in, and now someone was cooking onions. From the north end of the dining room where we sat down, the kitchen was maybe ten feet away. The dining room wall obscured almost all of the window where the runners would pick up food. The narrow hallway between the dining room and service window ran from east to west with a bathroom on both ends and server station in between.

Joe was seated with his back to the kitchen,

smiling at me and pointing his thumb back toward the source of the yelling. "Welcome! We do our best for that not to happen during service! Anyway, I think the best plan is to go over the menu, show you around the kitchen and downstairs, and just have you hang out for stories and whatever questions…you ever work in a restaurant?"

"No, I bartended for a little while, but that's it."

"I'll just assume you don't know anything, so don't let me piss you off if it sounds like I think you're stupid or something."

"No, no, that's fine," I assured him, "I know virtually nothing about back of house."

"Back of house!" he smiled, "You know back of house!"

Joe handed me The Five's menu; a simple 8.5x14 off-white sheet that listed choices for each of three courses.

The Five

3 Course Prix Fixe Menu- $45

Please choose one item from each course:

The Bad News Cafe

Soup and Salad

Spinach Salad with Warm Bacon Dressing and
Biscuit Croutons

Chicken Tortilla Soup

Kansas City Steak Soup

Appetizer

Chicken Liver Mousse- grilled bread, cherries,
pickled onions and Porubsky's pickles

House made Tagliatelle with Pork Cheek Ragu

Scotch Egg with G-Sauce Remoulade

Main Course

Hot Fried Chicken- 3 Cheese Mac and Cheese,
Marinated Celery Salad

Pan Seared Trout- charred scallion grits, fried
Brussels sprouts

Slow Roasted Salt and Brown Sugar Cured Pork
Shoulder- stewed new potatoes and green beans, cheese
biscuits

I've eaten more prix fixe and chef's tasting menus

than I can possibly remember, and with the exception of a railroad-themed restaurant in Lead, South Dakota, where mashed potatoes counted as a course, I had never seen anything quite like the selection at The Five. It was all food I'd love to eat or have cooked for family and friends, so maybe that was the focus. Tortilla soup was the one-off for me. I love tortilla soup, but I don't think I'd ever seen it on the same menu as house made pasta. The first thing I had to ask about after I got done reading it was the remoulade. "Joe...is the G-Sauce remoulade actually...."

"Go Chicken Go!" he blurted out. "I was going to toss your ass out if you didn't ask about that!"

"That's kind of genius," I told him.

Go Chicken Go is a local chicken chain best known for its fried gizzards and livers. The chicken is good, but nothing beats a mixed order of livers and gizzards. The original location is in the neighborhood where we grew up, and the G-Sauce that comes with each order is some combination of hot sauce, cocktail sauce, and relish I think. It goes on everything. You take one of their buttered rolls, make a little liver or gizzard sandwich, and dip that in the sauce or their mashed potatoes. I generally think less of anyone who doesn't love Go

Chicken Go. The G-Sauce is our hyper-local version of
Texas Pete, and seeing it as a remoulade on a local menu
made complete sense.

"I don't know what made me think of it, but I'll
feature it alongside something fried every once in a while.
It's best on fried shrimp. I make it into Kansas City as
often as I can, and my first or last stop is always Go
Chicken Go or Italian Delight for a calzone."

Italian Delight is another local spot where we
grew up, and their calzones are the equivalent of Go
Chicken Go's livers and gizzards. John's on Bleecker in
New York City is the only other place I've eaten a calzone
I love as much as Italian Delight's. Nobody else puts in the
correct amount of ricotta. Their pizza is also my favorite in
Kansas City.

"When did you guys move to Topeka? Italian
Delight had to still be in the mall, right?"

"Oh, for sure," he said. "We moved out here
when I was still in junior high, a few years before my
parents opened the place. I like to think that my folks
would appreciate my menu, but my dad would be
especially bummed that we didn't keep his sausage or
corned beef on there. He was old school, totally traditional

as far as his recipes and work ethic. The hot pickles from Porubsky's made it though! But you know what I mean? The only thing than worse than making a mediocre version of my dad's food would be if I ended up doing it better...when we went all new we went all new."

"I think you can have your own identity and still honor your family. What's going to bother you more," I asked, "not making his food at all or having to make it every day?"

"Exactly!" he agreed. "When it was my brother Tom and I running the place, maybe that could have happened. We didn't plan on ever doing it, but it wasn't off the table completely. But now, with my parents and my brother all gone – my brother being the real chef – with all of them gone I'm kind of at the limit of what I can do with food. I know I don't have a real chef's menu. I have what I can cook and I still need all of the help I've got to pull it off. So fuck it, you know? I cook what I like to eat how I like to eat it. There's some creativity, some is mine and I borrow the shit out of the rest, but it works for me and we have butts in seats every night."

"I would eat everything on your menu," I told him. And I meant it. "It's all familiar. Plenty of comfort in it, I'm assuming most of your customers key in on that immediately. My obsession lately is finding out why food matters, and I see some great examples. It's for us, local people will all get it."

"All locals. With some exceptions, obviously, but we don't have a big international following! I obviously go with the comfort food angle, but it needs to be memorable. I want to either tweak components in a way that makes sense or really develop specific flavor through repetition." Joe continued, "I also want stuff that's good enough to keep on the menu for a while. I can't think in terms of nightly specials or weekly menus. I admire the shit out of anyone who can do that, trust me. But I'll generally keep a menu for six or eight weeks before changing most if not all of it. The Kansas City Steak Soup never leaves the menu. That is the one constant."

Kansas City Steak Soup is something almost everyone I know grew up eating. It's not really steak soup, there's no steak in any version I've had. It's made with hamburger. It is very simple...roux, beef broth, browned hamburger, canned tomatoes, mirepoix and frozen mixed vegetables. It's cheap, easy to make and you can freeze it for eternity. My guess was that Joe made an exceptional version if it was always on the menu, but before we kept looking over the details I was curious about something. "Joe, I'm trying to think what would be the classic desserts with all of this...what do you guys serve?"

"We don't have dessert." He answered.

"No dessert?"

"Nope. We have a couple of dessert wines, some port, and cognac. But we haven't served dessert since my mom died. She made every dessert. I mean, we didn't even have it anytime she was too sick or out of town or anything, people just knew that was the deal. No dessert without her. She kept at it though, even after her cancer diagnosis. But the last pie was the last pie. It was my dad's call, so anyone who has a problem with it now? That shit's on the old man! If we weren't up for making his corned beef, there was no way in hell we were going to step into her shoes."

"Joe, you ever eat at The Bamboo Hut over in Independence when it was still open?"

"No," he said, "didn't make it out to Independence much."

"They had an awesome menu. Home style everything. And cheap. I guarantee you would have loved

48

it. Every appetizer was fried. Every single one. But they didn't have dessert either. The waitresses were all ballbusters. If you asked for dessert they'd just point at the bar. Drinks were cheap too. It was the best."

"Ha! I'll have to remember that...push the cordials guys!" Joe looked like he suddenly had a revelation. "Oh! I take it back, if someone really needs a baked good after their meal we can give them more bread! It's not listed on the menu, but one of my favorite things is our bread service. It's nothing big, just Roma Italian loaf with the sesame seeds and very cold butter. Specifically, Land O' Lakes Butter Continentals...the kind in the foil packets."

"Hell yes, classic."

"I'm weird about it, but I'm obsessive about keeping them as cold as possible without freezing them. When they get to the table they need to be rock hard. No reason, it's my weird thing. Soft, fresh bread, rock hard butter that you can't spread. You can't spread it so you either wait for it to get warm, which is for psychopaths, or you put two or three on your slice of bread and eat it like a sandwich. A butter sandwich. I get tired of my own food, but rarely a day goes by when I don't jam that bread and butter down into some boiling hot steak soup. The outside of the butter melts a little, but it's still cold on the inside, bread turns to mush. You cannot beat that."

"Oh my god," I was amazed, "what makes that good is what makes caramelized fat good."

I love to talk about food. Talking to a chef about food, down to the core of sense memories, textures, and our shared experiences is always the best of all possible worlds. Joe and I sat at the table until noon, going over each course of his menu. I still knew virtually nothing about the story I came for, but if I've learned anything in my relationships with people in restaurants it's the value of letting things happen organically. Joe lost his family in rapid succession and made the sacrifices for the business he inherited in the middle of the worst situation imaginable. If there was anything I could do, it was to encourage a chef to be excited about his food.

"People love the old-school spinach salad, I rotate that one in and out a lot. It's bacon on bacon, plus I cook the mushrooms in bacon fat first because raw button mushrooms are fucking disgusting. The red onion plus a little extra vinegar in the dressing cut through the fat. You need that, because on top of everything else are cheese biscuit croutons. There's your lesson in repurposing! My day-old biscuits become croutons, and I use my hamburger grease to make the roux for the steak soup." He continued, "Tortilla soup sounds weird, but who doesn't love tortilla soup? Right now it's the top seller as far as the first course, and it's good. That and the steak soup are proof that you have to make your own stock. Stocks and pasta. Those are two things with no shortcuts. My brother took a class on pasta making, and then he showed me. So part of it is sentimental, but..."

"Fresh pasta is the only way to go." I told him.

"Oh, what makes *my* steak soup unbelievably good is a gigantic dose of my demi-glace. I put a lot of it in there. *A lot* of it. It's a very basic soup, the original recipe doesn't even include seasoning. Why do your lips stick together when you eat my soup? There you go." Joe leaned way back in his chair, like he was trying to scratch his back or talk to the ceiling. "I do stuff I could eat anytime. Tortilla soup is a little weird, but you know what's even weirder and sells even better? When I make my hot and sour soup. A big bowl of fried wonton strips for the table. When a Chinese restaurant knows to automatically bring you the wonton strips, you feel loved."

"I think one big benefit of the food you're

making is the fact there isn't much of a theme," I told him. "Comfort food, basically. But way more than a mom and pop blue plate special."

"I'm not looking for continuity or a theme other than how the courses break down," Joe explained. "It's always soup and salad, a cold app, hot app and a pasta, then poultry, fish and either beef or pork for mains. I want people to get fed." He looked at me and asked, "You ever go to any of the crazy ass country restaurants like Lambert's?"

"I've never been to Lambert's, believe it or not," I said, "but we were down in Branson and ate at this place where the front of the building was a giant chicken decked out like Uncle Sam or something. Servers walked around with metal buckets full of fresh potato chips and fried pickles."

Joe put his hands on the sides of his head and pulled them away explosion-style. "Exactly! I'm not serving buckets of grease, but other than veggie lasagna we have portioned and frozen in case someone ask for a veg option, this isn't the place to balance your diet. And we don't sell it fast enough for it not to become family meal before it gets freezer burn, so I don't worry about it. And vegan food…to each their own but to me it's like a too skinny stripper shaking what she don't got. Anyway, I love those places where you pick your two sides and the choices are always fries, onion rings, mac and cheese, something like fried corn fritters, then *cottage cheese....broccoli*...what the shit? I'm either doubling up on the corn fritters or getting one order plus fries or rings, and I expect the staff to see that as the most normal thing in the world. Show me the dumbass eating broccoli with their patty melt!"

"Joe, what happened when you changed the format so drastically? I'm not assuming people from Topeka are any less knowledgeable about dining than Kansas City, but you went from patty melts and onion rings to chicken liver mousse and pan-seared trout. It couldn't have been universally well received."

"Well, we didn't lose any business after my mom died. Juric's stayed the same minus desserts. She wasn't here every hour of the day like my dad, and even less often after she got sick. But it was strange to have it just be 'the three boys' after she was gone, which is how she referred to us. Nobody was left who would overreact or run for a Band-Aid when you got burned or cut in the kitchen. Then when my dad had his heart attack we shut the place down without knowing we'd open it back up. It was never going to be Juric's again even if we kept everything exactly the same. My dad was a machine. We would have busted our asses to keep up with that pace and volume and watched it die a slow death. Tom was a legit cook, and I'd worked here enough over the years to have some idea what to do, but this was not our dream. It would have been much better to have mom and dad live a lot longer, sell the place and retire in Arizona or something. So part of it was practical, part of it was emotional, but we were going to give it a solid shot for two years and see what happened. There was no big revolt or controversy over the change. We kept some original regulars after the remodel and reopening, and we got new people because there's nothing else like this around here. We were getting by okay, but we never made it to two years before Tom died, so we never had that conversation."

The change in Joe's tone when he talked about his brother wasn't dramatic, but he slowed down. His words were timed farther apart, his eyes moving between the edge of the table and his bottle of beer. He picked up one of the menus, stood up and walked over to the bar. I couldn't see him but I heard the beer cooler open and a cap pop off a bottle. He came back over and sat down, his eyes on the menu.

"As far as the new menu being well received, it's good homemade food and nobody is leaving hungry." His voice was picking back up. "I'm not saying there isn't a place in Topeka for meticulously plated little bites, but this isn't it. Tom was a great cook, but his zone was the type of dishes we serve now. When your guests start to trust you and word gets around, then you can educate them a little bit...this is about the fourth time chicken liver mousse has been on the menu. Always with the hot pickles, that helps to sell it. I'm a massive fan of charcuterie, but a mousse or very simple terrine is my limit as far as cooking. Ironically, one thing that sells the mousse instead of a plate of pasta or a deep-fried fucking egg is a simple menu note I gave my servers. I figured almost everyone around here has eaten braunschweiger, just the regular grocery store stuff."

"Oh yeah, you either grew up on that or have no idea what the hell it is," I suddenly broke in, "but I'll still eat it. White bread, yellow mustard."

"But it's nothing like chicken liver, right? Flavor-wise no way. But as soon as people heard it's kind of like the stuff in the big yellow tube from the store, right next to the damn pickle loaf, it started selling better."

"Joe, no kidding here, the thing that sold me on my favorite restaurant on my first visit was a little jar of pork rillettes that reminded me exactly of Underwood Deviled Ham. The thin layer of fat, the texture, I went back to my childhood."

"Shit yes, deviled ham, Vienna sausages, Spam, Treet, canned corned beef," he started down the list. "A proud throwback to my people's packing house heritage. You mentioned wanting food to matter, well that food matters. I don't respect food snobs. They don't love food. They're the people who never took their action figures out of the fucking package, and I guarantee they are horrible at sex. The macaroni and cheese I serve with the fried chicken is unbelievable, people love it. It's a goddamn Diners, Drive-ins and Dives recipe. My cheese biscuits are a hacked Red Lobster recipe."

"Again, this is absolutely true, every year on my birthday we go to Red Lobster."

"Yes!" He actually stood up from his chair at the mention of Red Lobster. "When you were a kid you went to the one over by the Venture store, on State Avenue! How do I know that? Because it was the only fucking Red Lobster in our world. You got good grades that quarter! It was a celebration!"

I laughed out loud, I could have spent the rest of the day name-dropping local businesses from our hometown, but I just said, "You know how I can tell when I really love a dish? I immediately start thinking of ways to bastardize it. General Tso's tacos...there you go."

"You know how chefs are!" He sat back down, but stayed on the edge of his seat. "We keep horrible hours and eat the worst food. I have almost zero food in my house. I personally don't trust anyone who is too particular. I just don't. They are no fun, bad people to eat with. If I cook for you at my house, chances are good you're going to eat something like fish tacos made with fish sticks. Because they are delicious. And they are easy. I'm going to make some General Tso's tacos though, that sounds fucking good."

"Corn tortillas for those though, even the worst carryout Tso's sings in those. Flour tortilla with the fish sticks, right?" I asked.

"Oh, obviously." He faked total disgust at the question. "That's all for me personally, away from here. I genuinely want to make good food at The Five. I use quality stuff that everyone is familiar with, like Rancho

Gordo beans and Anson Mills grits, I get as much local meat and produce as possible. And I want to learn new things. I love rabbit but I've never served it, same with octopus. And perfecting a traditional cassoulet is something I'm working on right now."

"Rabbit is the perfect animal!" I said. "Nose to tail, liver, kidneys. If you could make them fat like a little pig that would be Nobel Prize worthy."

"I need to just throw one in the sous vide and go from there. Speaking of that, the yuppie crockpot is my favorite thing in the world."

That was a new one to me. "You call it a yuppie crockpot? That's hilarious."

"That's all it is!" He insisted enthusiastically. "But it has been a lifesaver for me. Prepping as much as I can ahead of time is the only way I can do it. Our fried chicken is basically Thomas Keller's Ad Hoc recipe, but I use only boneless thighs. I brine, sous vide and chill them, so all you have to do is bread them and cook long enough to crisp the crust. I started off with bone-in thighs, but the fat under the skin wouldn't render out enough and stayed a little flabby. Boning them out and trimming fixed a lot of that. Dunk them in hot sauce a friend of mine makes here in town, and boom."

He got up all of a sudden and walked the menus back to the host station, threw away his two beer bottles, and then came back and pushed in his chair. I took that as a hint to stand up.

"I could keep going, but I am way past time to check on the guys. Can't let World War Three break out. Oh! Crisp fish skin! That was my motivation to always have fish on the menu. I think I was in my thirties when someone served me properly cooked fish with crackly crisp skin. Just unreal. My school-trained cooks are better than me at it, but I've gotten pretty good. I was watching some show where Eric Ripert used Wondra flour on the skin of some sea bass, and I ran with that. That is a really good dish actually. Everybody is immediately drawn to fried chicken and the pork roast, but that fish with the charred scallion grits...and I dose the fried Brussels sprouts with hoisin sauce. It's solid."

Hunter S. Fatback

-3-

Joe led me through the bar to the kitchen entryway and said, "It's important to me that you understand first and foremost this is a restaurant. I'm not going to tell you how to report anything, but there are people working here who have a history with me and my family. My sous chef started as a dishwasher eight years ago after moving up from Mexico. My two new cooks are young guys out of culinary school and could work in a lot nicer places than mine. They're here because they want to be. My dishwashers, servers, bartenders...I've got everyone's back and they know it. Some I've known for a while, a couple are family friends, but it's like you've seen other places...yes Chef, no Chef, all that. This is my family business. My kitchen. You and I can fuck around all day like old friends, and I'm happy to give you that part of the story. You'll see what I mean though...I can be your buddy, I can be my staff's buddy, but when they talk to YOU it's going to be like you're a guest. That's respect...for me, the restaurant, I haven't had to teach that to anyone. You can learn any of the mechanics, but respect, loyalty, that's in you or it's not. You know what I'm talking about, don't you Mr. French!"

"Oh, I understand." And I did. "Whatever I write, you'll sound great, your place will sound great. I'm my only audience as far as that goes. I'm never going to be too familiar with you in front of your people... believe me, I get trust."

As if on cue, a man in a chef's jacket walked out of the kitchen towards the bathroom. He was probably in his late twenties or early thirties. His only acknowledgement of us was a glance and nod at Joe and a quick "Chef."

"Cesar, come over here!" Joe motioned him over to us. "Cesar, this is my friend Jerry I told you about. He's spending the day here, checking out what we're doing for a story. I'm about to take him downstairs, how are the guys doing?"

"Great, Chef. I'm about to get soup and cheeks going, shoulder will be ready early," he answered and stood there.

"So everything under control? You haven't had to scream at anyone for fucking things up?" Joe squinted at Cesar with mock concern.

Cesar flashed a smile and told him, "Just a minor correction! No harm done, nothing that can't be fixed. No hitting the new guy until next time."

"Thanks, I'll suit up around five or after, so you or one of the guys roll out family meal and just work with Tina on any notes for lineup. I'm here though, so come find me if anything comes up. And remember to always count to ten before you go into beast mode." Both of them chuckled at that.

"Will do, Chef. Nice to meet you sir!" And he was off.

"Cesar is a rock." Joe said with pride. "Plus with him around I don't have to be the bad guy every time. That's a guy who gets a bad cut, takes a cab to the urgent care so nobody has to leave work to give him a ride, gets stitched up and gets his ass back here. You don't teach that to people. And he's a dude who would feel insulted if he got back and I told him to take it easy. So, drinks on me after shift that night!"

From everyone I've met who works in a professional kitchen, injuries are taken in stride unless they are particularly brutal. If you can get the bleeding to stop with tape or Super Glue, you keep on working.

"Anyway, I like to think I'm an okay boss," Joe continued. "That's probably more of a relative thing in the restaurant business. I've never put my hands on anyone. The one guaranteed thing that will set me off is food getting cold, dying in the window. I've thrown some plates over that. There are a million little issues and fuck ups on any given night that can set you off, but that one is a constant. Whether you know nothing about food or you're some fucking Michelin star-chasing groupie, you know that hot food needs to be hot when it gets to your table, regardless of the restaurant. Things are running right and someone gives a shit. I'm usually the one doing expo, and everyone in the front of the house knows if I ask for a runner more than once or if god fucking forbid they see *me* run food, then there's going to be a discussion. And soup going into cold bowls. It pisses me off just thinking about it. And no music in the kitchen. I don't care about the prep kitchen, but upstairs it's never going to happen. I'm not running a fucking car wash. You got that info for free! How you doing? Getting a feel for things?"

"Yeah definitely. I have some familiarity with traditions from places where I'm a regular, but seeing your restaurant and the way you run it will help to round things out. I'm probably not going to include much operational stuff in my story, but I personally like it a lot."

"Oh, I know! Nobody wants to read about the shit cooks do with the other fourteen hours of their shift! We'll get to the sad guest story, it's an all-inclusive tour." He seemed suddenly annoyed. I wasn't sure if it was directed at me, people who would read the story, or maybe even the fact he would still have a full shift after we were done.

Joe gave me a quick overview of the kitchen; the pass, cold line, the line with sauté, grill and fry stations, oven, dishwasher and speed racks. All of it was pointed out unceremoniously on our way to the prep kitchen, but the smells of soups and that night's pork roasts were already filling the room. We went through a door near the opposite corner from the kitchen entryway and headed downstairs. The stairwell brought to mind gangster hideouts, every scary movie with a walk to the basement...an old wooden staircase with the steps anchored into crumbling concrete on both sides, the walls were a combination of unevenly placed stones that had been filled in during a previous decade with bricks, the stereotypical single naked lightbulb hanging from the ceiling. Before I had a chance to try and remember if I'd told anyone where I was headed that day in case I never came back, we reached the bottom of the steps and walked into a surprisingly large and well-lit kitchen.

The prep kitchen at The Five has a concrete floor and drop ceiling, and while it's large no space is wasted. The main room sits at the end of a short hallway to the left of the steps. Lining the wall on one side of the hall is a big Hobart mixer, a couple of stainless steel prep tables with a shelf on the wall above them that has an assortment of mixer attachments, sheet pans and cutting boards. At the end nearest the main kitchen is a deep prep sink. As I walked in I noticed fish fillets were in the process of being prepped on one table, and on the other sat a clear food storage container full of peeled hard boiled eggs and a bus tub partially full of raw, ground sausage. The opposite wall was lined mostly with a couple of storage racks with random cases of beer, canned tomatoes, bottles of G-Sauce, a box of onions and some of the staff's personal effects. Beyond those racks is the door to the walk-in, and lastly a large whiteboard with prep lists written out for "A.M" and "P.M.".

"One thing that I think should happen on *all* food TV programming that takes place in a professional kitchen," Joe began, "is a disclaimer to let you know almost nothing gets prepped and cooked one item at a

time. You would think that though, like oooooh every time
they make a dish it has its own little pre-measured *mise en
place*. That's a lot of fucking ramekins! Obviously the goal
is to keep anything that needs to be done a la minute to a
bare minimum. For this menu, right now you obviously
assemble salads, garnish your soups, cook your pasta, fry
your already prepped Scotch eggs and your sous vide and
breaded chicken, and you cook your fish as last minute as
possible. Keep hot stuff hot, cold stuff cold, your fryer and
your pasta water at temp. We're sending out a lot of the
same dishes at nearly the same time, so the smallest thing
can throw you off. Everything you can prep, cook,
portion, stock or store ahead of time is critical."

Joe's sudden switch into a slightly louder and
rhythmic voice made sense as soon as we walked into the
main kitchen. His prep cooks were out of view until we
came in and saw them both looking through the storage
shelves to the right of the doorway. He was politely giving
them a heads-up that a stranger was entering the kitchen.
The cooks could have been twelve or they could have been
thirty, standing there in their chef jackets, one with a
plastic container of bread crumbs and the other holding a
service-sized roll of plastic wrap. As old as I felt when I
met Joe, I felt even older. Both skinny with dark hair, one

a little taller than me and the other had a beard. They stood there silently until Joe spoke to them.

"Guys, this is Jerry, a friend of mine from way back. He's the reason I had you both come in early! He'll be hanging out with us for the rest of the day."

After a friendly but minimal greeting and introduction, they briefed Joe on where they were at with the daily work. Everything was on schedule for service with the exception of the trout and Scotch eggs I spotted when we came in. Joe asked if it had anything to do with Cesar yelling at them, and after one of them answered sheepishly in the affirmative, he told them to finish up and let him know when it was done. Then they'd all start moving everything upstairs to set up for service. While he talked to them I looked around the kitchen, stopping to read the prep list. I wondered what prompted the large header across the top that simply said "FUCKING LABELS!"

A.M.	P.M.
pull beef stock- walk-in	tortilla soup
demi- walk-in	cheeks

butts	thighs
chicken stock	roll pasta
pasta dough	mac and cheese
mousse- walk-in	beans-potatoes
bacon	cook mushrooms/scallions
dressing	fry tortillas
eggs	biscuits
fillets	bread
croutons	cure butts-overnight
mirepoix/onions (pickle-walk-in)	soak grits-overnight
	beef stock-overnight
clean spinach/sprouts	
burger	
remoulade- walk-in	
celery salad- walk-in	

When Joe finished talking to his cooks and came back over, I pointed at the board and asked him, "Does all of this prep happen every day? Is there some stuff you make ahead or freeze or anything?"

"As far as freezing, some pastas do well. Stock would be just fine but we go through it fast enough that any surplus only sits in the walk-in for two days max. There's some stuff that takes time, like anything labeled overnight up there...cure the butts, grits do better overnight but you can soak them same day. Chicken stock you can do same day, but we'll start beef stock as service is winding down and that simmers all night. Part of it is time but a big reason is that we need the burner space to cook. In the morning we'll pull it, drain, chill, skim and hold some back for demi. We don't have to do it every single day, but having too much is better than running short. Mousse, remoulade, Scotch eggs, anything pickled, pork cheeks are good for doing ahead and cryovacing...celery salad is always way better the next day...all those can be done ahead and FUCKING LABELED...you catch THAT? My guys are great, but when I spot a trend I give a solid warning shot first."

"HA! Kind of hard to miss, I was wondering what prompted that."

Much of what I've witnessed in kitchens would be viewed by a casual observer as bipolar at best with the insane teeter totter of emotion and reaction, such as a chef unloading on a cook and then high-fiving them two minutes later. Once service starts, the action is non-stop and there is a razor-thin margin of error. The real story of most restaurants is in the planning, prepping and organization, not necessarily the explosive frenzy on the line during service or the church-quiet fine dining ballet that people are used to watching in open kitchens or on TV. Joe's motive for the detailed review of his menu and operations became clear to me. It was a point of pride for him and everything we talked about was right in the zone of what I love to observe and learn from. It was similar to how chefs take pride in showing other chefs their walk-in. Joe had invited me into the belly of his restaurant during prep and relinquished all duties to his staff in order to spend time with me. I couldn't read his mind, but it was about more than an article for him. We were old friends, but we were never best friends. It may have been as simple as walking me through it to prove to himself he had really done it on his own. As the last member of his family, he had kept it going. So as far as my role, there was the story I came for and the story I was going to get. If they were still irreconcilable at the end of the day, I'd deal with it then.

With a $200 check and ten minutes of Facebook fame in the balance for me, I wasn't going to play annoying reporter with Joe. It was his house and I was his guest.

"We used to smoke a lot of weed down here!" He laughed like he just remembered it. "Mom was usually at the house working on desserts, and Dad was religious about having all of the prep work done and everyone out of here before service. We'd go down to the other end of the hallway and light up, and then either try to sneak out the back door or make a game out of doing whatever work we were supposed to do while we were high. The funniest thing was we were grown-ass men, not fourteen-year-olds. Tom had already been in the service and I was working my other job, but like a couple of children we'd fire up and try not to get caught. I think Tom did it mainly as revenge for the time our dad caught him trying to grow pot plants in mom's herb garden."

I laughed and asked, "He get his ass beat for that?"

"Actually, he didn't. I think our dad got depressed about Tom being stupid enough to think nobody would notice, like weed was going to blend in with my mom's chives. You never learn early enough in life that your parents are not complete fucking idiots."

It wasn't until he mentioned it that I realized Joe's dad spent all of those years working in that same space. Different methods and materials, but the same long hours and repetition day after day. I asked him, "How much of the stuff down here was your dad's?"

"That's a very good question. Some shelving here and there, the prep tables actually, but the big mixer is the main thing of value. It's special to me. He wouldn't let anyone else touch that thing, not even my mom. That was a huge point of contention for a while. He didn't want her in the way down here, and she didn't want him mixing any of her recipes. It would have been bedlam though with the two of them fighting over whether dough or sausage took priority."

Lots of the Croatian families I grew up with made their own sausage at home. Some even had small operations in their garage and a backlog of orders year-round. Men were usually in charge of sausage, and women who knew how to make it achieved fame by creating a dessert bread called povitica. Both of those things had a local following where everyone had their favorite chef, and because of the limited supplies sources were strictly for those in-the-know. Potlucks, parties and family gatherings were the preferred places to showcase the product from your secret source. With the high volume he had to produce and the years of practice, my guess was that Joe's dad made world-class sausage.

"Your dad do different types of sausage? Stick with one that was popular?" I asked.

Joe's eyes got wide and he said, "His kielbasa was unbelievable. I'm not just saying that because he was my dad, it was unreal. It was a religion for him. Way before people were talking about farm to table, he'd make me and my brother go with him as kids when he'd buy a pig and they'd slaughter it for him. It was pretty rough, made you rethink your relationship to food…until you ate the kielbasa. He could have made a business out of just that. Other old-school immigrants who knew what was good loved it, so that got more locals coming after it."

"So your dad helped start the early foodie movement!" I joked.

"I guess when you think about it that way! People weren't lined down the street like that crazy shit today, but he would always sell out of it. His corned beef was great too, and kraut. Jesus, there was a lot of action down here on any given day, heavy work…fat briskets going into brine, the meat grinder pushing out miles of sausage into casings, the wall of sauerkraut reek before someone took it upstairs. My folks packed the place out and never had to spend a dime on advertising."

"You get many of the new breed of foodies out here? Food tourists? I don't know if you have menu items people follow, but the place itself sounds like a big draw now."

"Oh! Yeah!" Joe laughed, and with no seating in the prep kitchen he just leaned back against a metal storage shelf and crossed his arms. "We do not get a ton of that. I guess since we have no web presence and nobody outside Topeka reads our paper, we've only experienced the minimum compared to chefs around here or Lawrence and KC. But word gets out, you're here right? It's just funny to me. I know from reading Yelp that people can be some entitled pricks, but that wouldn't fly here. At the same time, what's the worst that's going to happen with people who are genuinely fucking excited every time they go out? My cousin has a five-year-old, totally similar. Kid was like 'I'm Jimmy and I'M FIVE! I'M FIVE YEARS OLD!'…did that for two months after his birthday. I can wipe my own ass now mom and dad! Yeah! Foodies are like that. Look at *me*! I can *eat*! So you have grown adults living a loud five-year-old's birthday party right in front of you. It's fucking ridiculous, like getting a gold medal just for participating, but it's harmless. And you only see them for as long as you're worth an Instagram shot. Then they move on." He stood up straight, perked up like a lightbulb just went off. "You know what it reminds me of? You know how airlines have bereavement fares?"

"Oh sure," I said, "I used to work for an airline. Fielded pissed off calls about that all the time."

"So you know the deal, right? Well, the foodies I've run into are like people who think they are getting an inside deal if they can weasel their way into a bereavement fare. But they're just getting a discount on the highest possible fucking fare. They're the only ones who don't realize it, and everyone else who has a clue is just fine with it. They're going, 'I'm Jimmy and I'm five!' Well hey, live it up kid! Here's a goddamn sucker! The reality is, if you don't try and con some extras or recognition every single time, and you're just a nice person, once in a while you get upgraded to First Class."

"Joe, I honestly love your menu," I told him. I did, I knew I'd be back to try all of this menu and looked forward to finding out what was on the next one. "I would eat everything on there, have eaten almost everything on there for most of my life, but this is not the menu I'm expecting. In my mind I'm assuming it's going to be..."

"Death row goddamn meal!" he shouted, then laughed and stared at me like he was The Guesser and he just got my five dollars. "I've only had two reservations that stuck out, but it was the same thing both times. First, they don't just make a reservation like everyone else. They have to talk to the chef or owner, plus get a fucking email thread going, let you know they are kind of a big goddamn deal. They have a hundred fucking questions, and even though you know they've got money they fish for some kind of deal or a special menu that is just *theirs* so they can show off to their boring fucking friends. Never going to happen, the menu is the menu, but their money spends and no reason to be an asshole to them. Not my first rodeo with a whopping party of six bozos from strip mall country. They all want to ask me what my death row meal is, though. And even worse is when they want to tell me all about theirs."

"A friend of mine has a popular bar and people always call late on a Saturday and pretend they're coming with one of the Royals or Chiefs, so they need someone else bumped to make room for their party," I told him.

"Never had that happen. Tortilla soup may not have the same draw. I don't know exactly what they're expecting, but it ain't this. When every damn thing they eat has to contain some kind of revelation or be cutting edge with a retelling of the history, and it has to be photographed and discussed, rated and recommended while kissing each other's asses and vying to be the alpha foodie. This place here? My restaurant has to be like your race car hitting the fucking wall in turn four. Here's some hamburger soup kids! Wanna hear about the crack whore we found in the dumpster out back?"

"Did they bitch about it? Eat it?" I asked. A lot of people won't bring up issues when they're still in the restaurant. It would make too much sense, and they'd miss out on writing shitty emails to the owners or reviews for their friends. The people Joe was describing to me sounded like precisely the type.

"The folks I'm thinking about definitely ate it and they were polite, but my servers said they all deflated in unison and were visibly confused by the menu. Then when the food was exactly as it was listed, not some otherworldly version, they stared at each other like 'what the fuck' but ate it all. Of course, they required a visit from the chef, there's the awkward round of applause, and the questions…"

"Oh man, death row meal."

"Death row fucking meal. Look I realize I'm that guy now, but that's the most played-out topic I can think of. Awkward first date type of shit. People who don't know anything about food, it's the lowest form of conversation. And I don't think any of them found their new death row meal. At all. Nobody channeled their dead grandmother to bless my food. I just dodged the question. No answer would have been what they wanted. I wasn't going to start shouting *'Cuisine! Oh cuisine! You have my broken soul!'* and pull my pants down and show the scar where I cut my fucking balls off *for cuisine*!"

I laughed hard. I was probably that person at some point in my life. If not *that* person, definitely the asshole church member who can't take a hint that the restaurant needs to turn your table. One of the cooks stopped to tell Joe the fish and eggs were done, and that they had started carting their food upstairs. Joe would intermittently stop talking long enough to run over to the walk-in and pull out various containers that were destined for the kitchen.

"Oh shit!" Joe stopped in the middle of a trip back from the walk-in, a quart container of pickled red onions in his hand. "One of the death row crews...they had a guy with them who just did not fit in, and everyone was wondering what the hell was going on. It was obvious they were taking the restaurant's theme seriously though, but we never figured it out."

"What? He was dying or something?" I asked.

"Something like that...the group was all ladies except for him, and they were all dressed up like a suburban fashion magazine or something. The bossy soccer moms who make you want to kill yourself in line at the store. You had all these decked-out ladies who drove a good hour to get here, sitting with goddamn Ratso Rizzo."

"Maybe they were taking him to Bellevue!"

"He was going someplace, no place good. They were going on and on chattering away, checking in with him once in a while, but I swear to god everyone thought the dude was going to do a face plant at any moment. Fucking *Topeka Journal* would do their next story about some guy drowning in his soup while everyone else at the table was trying to get the perfect shot for Instagram. 'Oh! Pull Bob up and wipe him off! The chef is coming out! We can't miss a group shot with him!'"

He took his onions and continued going back and forth between the walk-in and the prep table closest to the steps, leaving a variety of containers and cryovac bags. Every couple of minutes, one of his cooks would come down and retrieve whatever was waiting for them.

It was almost 1:30, and even though I knew Joe and I were having a good discussion, I didn't want to get in the way of his employee's access to him if they were running behind. I've been around a lot of restaurants, but I'd never hung around a prep kitchen for any amount of time. Not that I haven't been curious, it is more a matter of not wanting to ask because I haven't had a legitimate reason to be there. The amount of work that has to get done in that space every day is hard to grasp, as is the sheer amount of equipment. At The Five, in the center of the room are two stainless steel prep tables set back to back for depth, with an industrial electrical outlet hanging down to within a couple feet of the table. There is plenty of room to walk around the tables, but not enough for any type of seating. Against one wall is a single deck convection oven and a tall speed rack, next to a storage rack holding baking pans, plastic containers, scales, food mills, pasta maker attachments, a stand mixer, robot coupe, a spice grinder and a knife rack. Against another is a mop bucket and a rack for brooms and dustpans. Other than that, every inch of every wall has a floor to ceiling stainless steel wire rack sitting in front of it. Storage bins of different flours and grains, baking powder, corn starch, cooking oils, syrup, vinegar, cooking wine, brandy and sugar line one wall. Around the rest of the prep kitchen are dozens of containers of spices, extracts, specialty sauces and oils, and plastic storage bins filled with potatoes, onions and garlic. I took mental notes of everything while Joe was busy.

He made his final trips to the walk-in to get a case of spinach and a case of Brussels sprouts, and he put them in the middle of the prep tables.

"So this is the routine every day?" I asked.

"Every day all day, from morning to night. One of a million little rituals you to go through when you're tied to a place." He smiled faintly and continued, "Other than the elephant in the corner – being the only one left in my family, I've got it about as good as anyone can. The building was paid for years ago, I have a great crew, and people keep coming here to eat. I'm not a chef but had to be one to keep this place going. Honestly, if my brother and I hadn't replaced Juric's with this, then I would have shuttered the building in a heartbeat when I didn't have him here anymore. Now there's some variety. It's all day every day, but compared to the same amount of work on a decades-old menu, this is heaven. My dad was built for it, Tom might have been built for it. I was the wild card after my dad died, I wasn't going to make one more fucking patty melt and have the millionth customer give me the same joke 'Oh, it was just *terrible*...har har har..I barely finished it!' Tom was up for doing something different if he knew I'd come onboard full time."

"What made the deal was a change of scenery, so to speak?" I personally could not imagine leaving a "normal" job to come and put in that much work for far less money. But I also couldn't imagine what it was like for Joe to be the last person anchored to the family business. That old building was the last thing all of them shared…all the milestones that must have taken place inside those walls through the years would lose the only other witness to their stories if he gave up and shut it down.

"That was it. I grew up on the food, I served and cooked the food, and my respect for my family being able to do the same thing for so long has grown dramatically now that it's my show." He leaned back against one of the shelves again, and from his standard crossed-arm position looked me in the eye. "The repetition is what you respect. You respect it, that ritual, more than the creativity. Dreaming up a menu or explaining your perspective about that menu is the fun part, and that's what people have in mind when they come in high off of an episode of 'Chef's Table'. They're imagining your Saturday morning chef trip to the farmer's market picking only the best stuff for service and dreaming up that evening's magical menu on the fly! The places with a format similar to ours, that's what I'm talking about. All the TV programming that's available now is great at selling cooking school to kids who will die before they pay that shit off. But it doesn't make cooks. Hitting the wall and sticking with it when you realize your life is a non-stop loop doing whatever the guy who writes the menu tells you to do. That's cooking. Will you end up being the guy writing the menu? Probably not. Will you be a household name? Definitely not. I don't know any fucking cooks who think in those terms, but hey more power to anyone who can!"

He paced a little bit, head down, arms still crossed in front of him. Silent for half a minute as he thought. I said nothing.

"Think about the kid in Chicago who is miles beyond any of his classmates from culinary school because he's in charge of filling those damn truffle explosions. It's good for a little bit, but before long his ass is praying for the next rookie to inherit that tiny piece of the machine and repeat, repeat, repeat. If he's *lucky* he'll get to be in charge of cooking a family meal within a year. He isn't collaborating with the chef on jack shit! That's at the highest level in this business, but being a cook is being a cook. Same thing but a different neighborhood, the guy who spends his nights making those goddamn flower onion things at Outback! Thank god for the onions! He can pretend the tears are only because of *those*! But there are crazy fuckers on both ends of that spectrum who thrive. Repetition can be comforting, it can be competition with yourself or others to sharpen your skills, or just straight up fucking endurance."

"Which is it for you?" I asked. "Is it one of those?"

He thought about it for a few seconds and said, "Comfort. But that...took a while."

Something about discussing the routine had a

noticeable impact on Joe's demeanor. His voice sounded heavier, he seemed more conscious of how he was painting the picture. After he answered my question he didn't make eye contact. He looked around the room quietly and walked over to pick up an empty flour bin and a five-gallon bucket, walked them over to where I had been standing the whole time and turned them into makeshift seats. I had a sense of anticipation like a kid whose dad was about to lecture him or tell him what it is to be a man. We both sat down. Joe leaned down and looked like he was staring at the concrete between his feet for a moment, then he sat back up and looked me in the eyes.

"I came in early this morning to chop the mirepoix, so it would be done before you got here. I have only missed doing that maybe three times since I reopened The Five. It needs to be imprecise, because I have the worst knife skills of anyone in my kitchen. That's my time alone down here every day. It's my ritual right after walking in the front door. That's for the Kansas City Steak soup. I don't give a shit who does it for any of the other dishes, but that batch is mine and everyone knows it. We don't have to talk about it. I don't tell anyone. Cesar can do that if there's a new guy. I need to see my shitty mirepoix in that soup every day. That's my anchor."

He continued, "When my brother died, this place wasn't even a thought. There wasn't some decision to reopen or not. Losing your mom to cancer, your dad to a bad heart, that's horrible but you know that's how things happen. Tom was the rock here. He was my friend my whole life, knew me before I was born. My big brother. Neither of us had any idea if The Five would be a success, but at least there were two of us, you know?" I could tell from the way that he spoke that this was hard for him. He was speaking to himself as much as he was to me, and the blankness in his stare that would come and go told me that he was beginning to feel the memories. I imagined he had put a lot of thought into how to tell the story between our first conversation on the phone and this talk between the table and the bake shelf.

"Jerry, you ever pick out a casket?" he asked.

"Yeah. I've done that."

"Funeral people are just salesmen. You want to believe they empathize, but they upsell you on every little thing. My parents took care of all of that stuff for themselves, prepaid all the funeral details, all the burial. When it was Tom, it was just me and this fake sorry

87

funeral director telling me I needed some vault with lining where my brother's casket would go, because the cheaper vault could leak water. Like that mattered. It went on like that for three fucking hours...the casket, the registry book, the bulletins, if you want a free obituary on their website or a personalized one you pay for, a giant itemized bill you take to the front desk like a doctor's office. You're ready to agree to anything just to get away. I took the bag of all of Tom's personal effects that they gave me, and I sat in my car with no clue where to go. I couldn't go sit at my house. I needed to go to Tom's house to pick out his clothes, but my mind couldn't even go there. So I came here, and I stayed here for three days until I had to go to my brother's funeral. You want a Coke?" he suddenly stopped and asked. "I'm going to have another beer."

He ran upstairs to get our drinks, and I sat there absorbing where the shift in his story was going. Joe went from an overview of Operations 101 straight to his gut. Whatever happened to create the local legend of The Five started at the point Joe had begun describing. His family and all of their work in that restaurant became real to me; more than a story or curiosity. My insistence that I always tried to make my dining routines about the people I met and friends I made would be hollow if I didn't allow for the same emotional connection with Joe.

He was back in less than two minutes, and stayed with it. "After about a day of just sitting upstairs I texted a couple of people to let them know I was ok. It'd be a dick move to just disappear. I found out later that my dad's friends you read about in the paper went over to Tom's house and got clothes to take to the funeral home. They reached out to all of our family and friends, whatever regulars they knew from here, and gave them the service details. I didn't even remember I had started writing the obituary at the funeral home, but I guess I did because they finished that and sent it in. I stopped off at home long enough to take a shower and put on clean clothes before the funeral, but other than that I was just here...didn't eat, didn't fall down into a drinking binge. I'd put on music and lay down on the banquette for who knows how long, took a few phone calls. And then I went to my brother's funeral. I just went on autopilot dealing with the people. The only thing I remember cutting through all the numbness was right after I got there I was standing out in the lobby with one or two other folks before the chapel opened up. I heard someone say 'Tom's here'. For maybe one second I had that feeling like you do when you're waking up from a dream, like the whole thing had just been a nightmare, it jolted me. But they were just telling one of the family that they'd moved him into the chapel and we could go in."

Between my own history and working in ministry when I was younger, I have an unusual amount of experience with funerals. There isn't a role I haven't had to take on more than once. It's easy to forget how unnatural and artificial the experience can be, and what grief feels like when you are trying to make a social hour out of the entirety of someone's life.

"A bunch of us came back here after the service. Because there's a bar now. People got hammered, told stories, the usual stuff. Little by little, people would check in with me to make sure I was going to be okay, then they'd leave. I still had no plan or idea what to do. So here I sat. That was a Monday. I still hadn't eaten anything. I wasn't hungry but I knew I needed to start getting my shit together, and starving wasn't going to help my brain any. I came down here and looked all around, went through the walk-in seeing what might be good to cook and what had to be thrown out. Looking back, I don't know why it didn't occur to me to go out and get dinner. But I had something to focus on, after days of nothing."

He stood up for a moment to stretch and take another sip of his beer. "We always had beef bones for stock, so I started there. When I saw how much produce was starting to go south, I put in two more roasting pans of bones and started the longest onion, carrot, and celery chopping marathon of all time. It was insane. No robot coupe, I just went at it. When the bones were done I got our two biggest stock pots going. I figured after smelling stock for the rest of the night I'd be hungry enough to figure something out. I ended up dialing in on the steak soup, there's no way I wouldn't eat that, it would be like medicine. The most familiar of all comfort foods for me. I would always be hungry for that no matter what. I had to run out for bags of frozen vegetables, but other than that we had everything I needed to make a freakish amount of this fucking soup. Our biggest stock pots, the ones you saw when we headed down here? I ended up with one completely full and one about halfway."

"That is a ton of soup. It had to be a good break for you to just focus on the task," I said.

"I wasn't even thinking in terms of meals or freezing it... I think I was mentally preparing to clean the place out and sell it. It was early that Tuesday by the time I got the stock done and soup going. Not an ideal breakfast, but by that time I was hungry. The problem was my brainstorming and massive project was all done. I ate some soup. So what then? Before I slipped back into my coma, in walks Cesar. Like it was a normal Tuesday morning. Didn't say shit except for 'Morning Chef.' He cleaned the bar where everyone was drinking the day before, swept, mopped. The kitchen upstairs probably looked like a bomb went off, even worse down here. He got all of it. Did the dishes, packaged up the full pot of soup and put it in the walk-in. He got the place in order, top to bottom. Then he grabbed a bowl of soup, and sat down and ate at the table next to the one where I was sitting. We never said a word. Around noon or so, my two cooks at that time came in. Same thing. Like a normal day. They went off into the kitchen and downstairs. No clue what busy work they found to do. Then they came out and ate and nobody talked. That's how it went for the rest of the day. I assumed Cesar got on the phone and told everyone to get their asses to work. Servers, bartenders, hostess, dishwasher, I don't have a big crew. They all came in. They all ate Kansas City Steak Soup. It was the definition of comfort food. The silence thing was getting weird I guess, so at some point my bartender Moira turned on some music. She's still here, so is our hostess Tina who never shuts up. Once she started chattering away then it seemed more normal. I was so fucking gutted. In hindsight, I was much worse off than I let myself realize. My family was gone, but I'd taken for granted what these people mean to me. And I sold myself short on what I thought they felt about me. Some stuff goes so deep there's no thank you that makes sense. I think I owe them all my life."

Anyone who has spent time in or around the business understands the complete trust and complete dysfunction that comes from working under pressure in close quarters night after night. The laughter, tears, anger, hazing the new people, constantly saying goodbye to friends as their lives change and they move on…all of those things happening in parallel to creating hospitality for strangers. The story Joe was telling me was amazing but not surprising.

He stood back up, stretched his neck from side to side a few times and went back to leaning against a corner of one of the shelves. "Everybody did that every single day for a week. Everyone came in, cleaned and set up as much as possible with no customers and no menu whatsoever. Me and the cooks took turns piecing together a meal for everybody from what we had on hand plus odds and ends from the store. We never really closed, and we never really opened back up. I guess they took my lead…I am not hard to read mood-wise, so as I lightened up someone would have a significant other show up around dinnertime. Or one of their kids. It was a process over a few weeks. The longest, most unintentional soft reopening with friends and family night after night. The till started ringing again with people buying drinks, my servers got tipped. Then an actual menu started to form because enough people were coming in, and on it went. We just made food everyone liked. That's it. One night one of my servers had a family friend whose house burned, so that family came here every night and we fed them. Within a day or so of that, one of my dad's friends lost his wife, and he became even more of a fixture. The timing of things was terrible in such a short period for people we all knew, and we had food for them."

"So that was it. That's what started it." I said.

"THAT is what started it." He replied. "The chef who hosts the sad and the grief stricken. It's fucking crazy how things work, huh? So the mirepoix is mine every single day. And the steak soup never leaves the menu."

-4-

We headed upstairs for a change of scenery and some fresh air. The kitchen was in full swing. All burners were in use...beans and potatoes stewing in one pot, pork cheeks braising in another, cheese being stirred into a roux, mushrooms sautéing. Pasta was being rolled out on the counter right under the window where servers would be picking up their dishes. Fresh tortilla strips were sizzling in the fryer. The smells were beautiful. One of the cooks was on his knees in front of some open drawers in the low-boy, rotating containers from the back to the front and making room for everything from the walk-in that had been stacked on top. The dishwasher was scraping and scrubbing sheet pans. A professional kitchen has an economy of movement that does not easily accommodate extra, unexpected bodies. I let Joe take the lead and I followed his steps like we were headed through a minefield. He walked to the corner straight across from the basement entry and opened a door that led outside. There were no steps or porch, just a three-foot drop to the ground. He hopped down and walked toward the parking lot, and I did my best to jump down without blowing out a knee. He took a seat at the picnic table I spotted when I first pulled up.

"This is where the staff comes for a smoke or to take a break. It's like the neighborhood stoop in a movie or something, people driving by spotting the bad kids out here. You smoke?" he asked as I was about to sit down.

"Not cigarettes anymore, I've been into cigars for a while. Before I started all the fine dining, actually."

"You bring some with you?" I was surprised how much he perked up at that. Like I said I'd brought a bag of weed to the drive-in.

"Oh, I'm in pocket, bro. I'm holding. You have to maximize your cigar time. You like cigars?"

"I'm not an aficionado, but I have one from time to time. If you don't mind...." he smiled and put his pack of Vantage cigarettes back in his pocket. I didn't know they even still made those.

I walked to my car and grabbed a couple of Partagas Serie D #4's, then clipped and lit them both on the way back over to the table. That's a common courtesy if you aren't sure about someone's familiarity with the process. He had come around to the other side of the table, sitting facing out at the parking lot. I took a seat next to him.

"These are from a box from 2013, good year for them. A favorite in my rotation, good price, consistent," I told him.

"Cuban?" he asked.

"Yeah. I've always got to be into something not totally legal, but I'm also a family man! Can't be going to jail!"

He laughed. We sat back and enjoyed the breeze on a strangely warm afternoon, taking draws from our smokes. It was quiet except for the passing cars, and intermittent pounding or drilling from a body shop up the street.

"You know Jerry," he began, "I was trying to remember the last time I even saw you. We knew a lot of the same dudes, Stevie obviously, but never really hung out much outside of school. And I moved before everyone could drive. Going way back to grade school you were one of the smart, spelling bee, nerdy kids. Then by the time I started coming back for visits in high school, you were some kind of fucking acid-eating, bomb-making, drunk delinquent. And you had way older friends. Right?"

"Well Joe," I told him, "I found out pretty quickly

that you can be the fat kid in Chess Club and get tormented, or you can be the fat kid who cheats death from alcohol poisoning, and can blow up a car. Nobody torments that fat kid. You don't learn none of that shit matters until way too late."

"No shit! I was just starting Junior High when we moved. I'd come back into town from time to time for different stuff, family events, whatever. I was either a junior or senior the last time I saw you, I think."

"Yeah? Hell, that opens up a whole lot of possibilities for the circumstance..."

"It was at a party. One of those all ages music clubs out on State Avenue. Tom and I both came back one weekend, he knew someone in a band who was playing it. A bunch of the guys were there."

"Wow. No recollection. Anything different about it?" I asked.

"You remember Black Jerry? He always wore that fucking Journey shirt?"

"Oh yeah. I remember Jerry." I knew where this was headed. I hadn't thought of it in years. There were two of us named Jerry in our circles of friends, the other one was referred to as Black Jerry so people would know which one they were talking about. He was black. For all I know, whenever I wasn't around everyone called me White Jerry or Fat Jerry. Nobody ever thought to just call us by our last names. He was a soldier. Up for whatever. Good or bad.

"The last time I saw you, you and another guy were trying to pull a bunch of fuckers off of him, it was brutal."

"That did not go very well. Jesus. That was a bad one. He walked away from that. I don't know anyone else who would have. I sure as hell wouldn't," I said.

"What set that shit off? He was a decent dude as far as I remember, never fucked with anybody."

"He was black."

"No shit? Goddamn." He seemed genuinely shocked. "You forget shit like that is real, which is fucked up in itself. And where you and I lived...it's not like you could afford to be too fucking racist, not in public anyway."

I would end up seeing far worse things in my life, but the incident Joe brought up was one of those moments you reflect upon as you get older and your universe expands beyond a thirty block stretch of your hometown. Brutal violence is rarely, if ever, like the movies. First of all, there's no space, no buffer between you and the blood and sound. And things happen way faster in real life. I don't remember what set it off, but Jerry made the mistake of mouthing off to a group of guys and then hitting back when he got hit. He was black, so resistance was all six white guys needed to jump on him. Me and one or two other friends jumped in to help him. Not because we could look into the future and suddenly understand how racism or white privilege impacted the world around us and constantly provided learning moments, it was simply because assholes were beating on our friend. I don't know how many times they pounded his head into the concrete before, out of pure luck, one guy I pulled off of him fell hard and split his head open on a steel beam that held up the awning in front of the building. That injury stopped the action long enough for us to pull Jerry out of there. The guys who instigated it looked at me like I was the wet blanket telling looters to stop the free-for-all...who would dream to ruin an opportunity to beat on a black kid? After three decades, the single thing that sticks out the most was how Jerry jumped up to show he was okay. His head split open badly enough that I wouldn't have been shocked to see skull, blood and sweat pouring, in a daze and acting like he was the one who screwed up.

We sat for a couple of minutes, quietly smoking our cigars. If I hadn't just reconnected with Joe for the first time in years earlier that morning, the natural joke to play on him would have been to sarcastically thank him for mentally recording Jerry's beating instead of jumping in to help. That would have snowballed into him busting my balls out of pure shame, or both of us sitting there counting all the ways we'd solved racism since high school. Before long Joe was back at it, digging up another, albeit less traumatic, blast from our completely clear in hindsight past. "Hey! Remember Wyandot Swim Club?" He was suddenly excited.

"Yes, Joe. I remember Wyandot Swim Club. While you're in the Wayback Machine you run across any lynchings? I know somebody at Channel 9! If the chef gig doesn't work out you can be the racist history correspondent or some shit!"

Joe was laughing out loud, giddy to be fucking with me. Wyandot Swim Club was where almost everyone I knew who could not afford a membership at Victory Hills Country Club, was a member. That is to say, everyone I knew who was white. It was completely segregated; no black people were allowed to become members. And this was happening at least into the late Eighties. I can't remember when it closed down. People still wax nostalgic about the place, it was a pretty nice swim club. There is a whole social media group dedicated to it. But if you bring up the "Whites Only" aspect, much of the time they either stop talking and drift off into space like nothing was said, or they get very defensive. "It was NOT segregated! It was a PRIVATE CLUB! Membership was decided on a case-by-case basis! Why do you have to bring that up? I was a lifeguard and I didn't even SEE color if someone needed help! You're just TRYING to be hurtful!" People who were around for it still get worked up about it today, in 2017. But I promise you, when the Jackson Victory Tour came to Arrowhead Stadium in 1984, there was a 100-percent "Whites Only" swim club in Kansas City, Kansas, where they would not have been welcome.

Joe was finally starting to calm down a little bit. "I'm sorry, it's not funny, but I would torture my parents with that every once in a while as an adult...mom and dad how could you have taken part in that! It's just awful! 'Oh Joey! We didn't realize...it was so different then....' I would finally let them off the hook, but damn there's just no defense unless you're going to go full-blown racist, so it's perfect to fuck with someone."

"Yeah, I do the same shit with mine." I said.

"So whatever happened to the other Jerry?" he asked.

"I don't know. Dead more than likely. I heard from someone he did a stretch out in Lansing, I don't know what for. The main guy who jumped him shot and killed himself a year or so later. One of the dudes who tried to help him is STILL in prison. You and I made out like rock stars."

"I think moving out here did me a lot of good. Knowing you were coming out kicked off some trips down memory lane. Before my mom passed, I'd only known one other person who died. I was fifteen and my whole family came back to KC for the funeral...you remember that kid Arnold? He was riding with some older dude who was drunk and crashed, they both got killed. Drunk driving was the new big thing, M.A.D.D. and all that."

"I knew both of them, actually," I answered.

"That was my first funeral. It was sad, and strange for a kid when it's another kid...you don't think of death that way. What I remember most were these fucking girls from the drill team, cheerleaders or something...fucking weeping and making a scene. Not one of us, including Arnold, had said five words to girls like that in our lives. A totally different league, way off limits."

"I know I sure as hell didn't," I said.

"But it was a chance to get into some drama, some tragedy whoring. That still sticks out. Because you still see shit like that all the time."

Joe was quiet for a minute. He took another puff from his cigar, looked at me and said, "You KNOW those little bitches grew up to be foodies."

We went back and forth like that for a little while, catching up on random details from our lives. We shared histories with so many of the same people and places, but very little with each other. It's always a game when you meet someone from the old neighborhood...a friendly trivia match that goes back and forth faster and faster until someone doesn't remember a specific person, place or event. Everyone remembers Smak's Hamburgers, BUT do you remember how many of them there were, details of the menu, or what the mascot was? What was the worst fight you ever saw at a Croatian wedding reception down at the old Armory building? Where did your crew prefer to hold their illegal drag races? Who really went to see Ozzy when Randy Rhoads was still alive and who was full of shit? Concert attendance was the most heavily vetted topic of all subjects anytime the back-in-the-day discussions took place. If you were old enough to remember a time before line numbers when you had to camp out overnight for concert tickets at Capers Corner, that gave you a great advantage. That is, until someone waded into the conversation who was old enough to remember the universally panned performance by Led Zeppelin at Memorial Hall...at that point you may as well just quit speaking. It's never just about the power of your memory. The critical detail is always how you tell the story. Style counts for everything. I imagine there is a similar custom in every town and every culture that exists, but for the purposes of two middle-aged guys from the Midwest, Joe had very good style. I was hoping we'd be back at it again sooner than later, because we were getting close to the middle of the afternoon and I knew he had a business to run. I wasn't making headway with my story, but I was having a good enough time reconnecting to not care.

"Oh man, Jerry, here's one before we head back in. Not from back home, this was about a year ago. Totally fucked up." He sat up straight, coughed and tossed his cigar butt into a coffee can on the ground next to the picnic table.

"What happened?" I asked.

"We had a guy come in one night right as we were opening, like 5:35, and he walks in by himself." The way his normally casual tone and delivery slowed down and became more deliberate, I was intrigued. "I was in the back with the rest of the cooks, servers and everyone were out front doing their stuff. Moira, the lady who manages my bar, was finishing setting up and the dude walks in completely shitfaced. The drunk for days, how is this guy getting around, level of shitfaced. Usually we'll have two of my dad's friends fucking waiting to get in the door, but no other customers were in yet. He takes a seat in the middle of the bar and just sits there, not saying anything, just staring straight ahead. Moira goes on about her business for a few minutes, waiting the guy out to see what happens. You'll meet her in a little bit, she's great but not a big smiling 'Welcome! What can I do for you today?' type of person, she's Russian, you'll see what I mean.

Anyway, there was no question this guy was NOT going to be drinking here, but she asked how she could help him. She was the only one in there with him, so this is her telling what happened, but he said something like 'I hear this is the place I go if I'm having a bad day! I AM having a bad day! I wanted to come here and have someone make me a drink before it gets worse!' Strange for it to be that early in the shift, but nothing outside the typical drunk redneck banter. The main concern would be having his ass hang around long enough to try and make friends with strangers at the bar, jabbering about his bad day. Moira gave him the usual 'I'm sorry you're having a bad day, I'd be happy to make you a drink but I think you've had enough alcohol' speech, which would normally just get a 'Fuck YOU, I'm leaving!' and off they'd go. But not this guy. He puts his hand way up and BAM brings it down on the bar hard enough for me to hear it back at the pass, and tells her 'I want a drink! NOW!' So she tells him she'll talk to her boss, runs back here and gives me the 'fucking get out here' look. She had never done anything like that before, so I knew something was off."

He continued with his story, "I didn't do any of the mediation you do when it's the owner's turn to come out and deal with a shitty customer. We were right at the

107

start of our shift, work still needed to get done, and there was zero chance anyone was babysitting this dipshit. I told him hey, you've already had too much to drink, my bartender has refused to serve you, and now I'm asking you to leave. He went back into the 'I heard this is where I come when' blah blah blah, and I stopped him and said, 'I don't know what you heard, but you're drunk and you are leaving. I can call you a cab, because I don't think you should drive.' That's the hint you drop before you invoke the *cop* word. But he didn't move. The fucker turned to me and gave me the 'fuuuuuuck youuu' normally reserved for the bartender."

"Oh man, I'm always telling my friends back home it pisses me off when I show up too late or leave too early and miss shit like that," I said.

"This was one of those weird but not outside the realm of reality situations. Yet. I was pissed off but I wasn't going to get physical with the guy. It's a bad example, you're liable if he gets hurt, and with rednecks out here you can't tell if they're one of those country strong fuckers who will rip you in half. And if I had to call the cops, then he's here until they show up and getting all the details from him and us, while customers are coming in....just a nightmare."

"You've come a long way, Chef. A man of restraint," I joked.

"Yeah, that's me alright! I took one last shot at getting rid of him. I said he isn't staying in my restaurant, I could call a cab for him, or I could call the police, but it was time for him to leave. Nothing. Fucker just sits there fuming, looking in the fucking mirror behind the bar. Then no shit, as if by a literal miracle, two cop friends of ours stroll in for a drink after their shift. My parents were always friends of law enforcement, and uncharacteristically for guys like me or you...especially you... I've kept that family tradition. No politics, no agenda, they are people we have known for as long as we've lived in Topeka, and I have a decent quiet spot. When you own a business, you can do a lot worse than know some police. But anyway, they walk in, the drunk asshole sees them in the mirror, stands up and boom he's out the door in one second. Moira and I relayed some of the story to them, but he was already gone when they went out to make sure he wasn't hanging around. But the important detail here is, me, my bartender, and two local cops could all attest to the fact that the guy was drunk when he got there, belligerent, but was not served any alcohol."

"What the hell happened?" I asked.

"What the hell happened was...the guy leaves, and fifteen minutes later he is at his house, and he fucking murders his wife and he murders his best friend who he assumes has been sleeping with his wife."

"What in the fuck?"

"What in the fuck is correct. And this is a god's honest, no bullshit, no embellishment, thing that happened."

"Were they fucking around, the guy and his wife?"

"No idea," Joe said, "there was the usual coverage in the paper but it didn't get more than a day, some school bus accident or something knocked it out of the rotation. I talked to the cops who walked in when he was here, and they didn't have any details other than he went berserk. The paper always says shit like death by gunshot, which he definitely shot them, but I guess it was a horror show. Really bad stuff. Guy confessed too, so there wasn't any drawn out trial."

"That is one of the craziest things I've ever heard. Jesus. Normally someone gets wrestled out the door, whatever. Damn." I was shocked, I did not expect that ending.

"It was horrible, that fucked us up for a little while around here. And as shitty of a thing to have happened, I feel bad even saying it out loud, but you have no idea how thankful I am..."

"That you didn't serve him! Oh my GOD!" I said, finishing his thought.

"Yeah...yeah. That would have been it for this place. And for me. I would have said fuck it, got my old job back and never thought about this place again. Moira would never serve a drunk like that, she doesn't even like serving you if you're sober. But oh my god, if I had a new bartender or something, or someone wanting to placate that asshole just to shut him up. From then on it would have been "When you absolutely, positively have to murder your wife and your best friend, you have GOT to stop by The Five first for one last cooool and crisp martini!"

"Oh man, that would have stayed in the paper for a while." It would have been an urban legend for decades.

Joe was a little dazed just talking about it. "God, it would have been even worse if the guy actually made a reservation, came in totally normally for dinner and *then* went and did it....in court he'd go, 'Your Honor, I did kill my wife, but I would not have had the strength to do it had it not been for the hearty meal I enjoyed from Chef Joe Juric, at The Five restaurant, just off of Northwest Topeka Boulevard! I was very meticulous with my Yelp review and photos of my meal! I throw myself before the mercy of the court...'"

I sat there shaking my head, "Damn Joe. I don't know what kind of bartender school or liability training they put you through in Topeka, but you would have been one of those multiple-choice questions on the test. When a customer staggers into your establishment already intoxicated, do you A) refuse service, B) serve them but ask for their car keys first, or C) question them about their domestic situation and after receiving a verbal confirmation they are *not* planning to murder their wife, serve them but maybe only beer."

"Only beer...nice touch, man." He snapped out of wherever it was his mind had gone. "Stuff like that reminds you of what a weird place your restaurant has become. We do nothing to intentionally cater to people with some kind of hardship, other than a couple of pieces in the paper it evolved totally organically. But you forget the legend, gimmick, whatever it is, because you're ass deep in work running the place and serving food like any other restaurant."

"Nothing ever came of that in the paper? Did any customers ever ask about it?" It was strange that something so magnificently horrific didn't get more attention in a town that size.

"Nothing at all. It probably would have if the next couple of days were thin for big news, but it was just us and our cop friends. It did stick with us here for a while, that's a real scare. If he was pissed enough to kill someone, why not start here? Was that his original intent before the police walked in? It spooked us. I still feel guilty for not doing more, calling the cops, or anything that would have slowed him down. It might have made the difference."

"Or he just could have killed you instead," I said.

"The only other thing we found out was that they had kids. I joke about the whole thing because I'm fucking broken, but he had taken his kids over to his mom's house earlier so that they wouldn't be around. So you've got kids now with no parents who lost them in the ugliest way imaginable. The dad's alive, but he's never leaving prison. Hell, we lost our parents years apart as grown ass adults and it shook the hell out of us. What happens to kids after that?"

"I...don't know," I answered, shaking my head, "It's the same as a suicide. Leaving people behind to deal with that shit forever."

"It's cowardly shit. Now we're way more sensitized to people making reservations. You don't want to play counselor. Ever. I've got food. I think it's pretty decent food. But that's all it is. You eat it. It makes you feel good. A day later you take a dump." Joe stood up and held his elbows at chest height, twisting his body as far as he could in one direction before reversing the stretch and heading toward the front of the building. "And on THAT note...time to get inside. We'll hang out up front, all is well in the kitchen. Sitting out front before service will be fun, people won't know how to act. I get to yammering and lose track of time."

"Oh, me too." I said. "We've covered a ton of ground. I can always come back out."

"Hey, I saw Moira pull up across the street a little while ago," he told me. He stopped walking and turned to face me. "Like I said, you'll see what I mean as far as demeanor, but along with Cesar and Tina she's my other rock around here. She was a nurse for a while in Russia, and originally just waited tables part-time for my parents. She ended up caring for my mom after she started getting too sick to get around on her own. Us guys would do what we could, but having another woman, a nurse, for her made so much of a difference. I have a lifetime bond with her after that, like a mean aunt, but she is not a great bartender. We just didn't know what to do with her after my folks were gone. She was *not* going to be a fine dining server. The bar was a new addition, we had no clue if anyone would even care about it, so we thought what the hell…see what happens with her as bar manager."

"Is she a problem with customers?" I asked him. "I understand the bond, but stuff like that can kill your business."

He laughed and threw his hands up. "That's the thing. She busts ass, and people really like her. Maybe I'm too close to her so I don't get it, but some people take it like she's one of those fake shitty and mean employees at a Fifties-style diner and eat it up. If they're taking too long she'll tell them 'You need a whiskey' or whatever, and ninety-nine times out of a hundred they go with it. Then you've got the people who like to ramble non-stop to their bartender about their problems and whatnot, and when she finally says *anything* to them it's not even ten syllables, like 'Life can be hard.' They're drunk and take it like she's some kind of sage...'Yes, that's it, life *can* be hard...it *can* be, but not always...' So they're fine with her too. Maybe it's the accent, no idea."

"Hey man, if it works it works," I said.

"She doesn't know you, so why don't you head in first and tell her you heard this is the place you go when you've had a bad day!"

"Are you serious?"

"No...I am not serious. It would be funny to me because all I do is bust her chops. But not to her. And definitely not for you."

-5-

We headed back inside through the front door of The Five. Joe went to check on the kitchen and I visited the men's room. I don't think it has seen much renovation since the days of Juric's. Clean and tidy, but reminiscent of a wood-paneled bathroom you'd find in someone's basement rec room. When I walked out, Joe was already sitting at the bar drinking a can of Coke. I knew a few beers probably hadn't affected him, so I assumed that was about being an example for front of house, but didn't bring it up. As I was walking over to have a seat, a lady carrying a case of Miller High Life bottles walked out of the bathroom I was just occupying and carried it behind the bar. She was probably ten or so years older than me, slightly shorter, wearing a black, short-sleeved collared shirt and jeans, her dark hair pulled back in a ponytail and sporting a pair of black Dansko's. She was all business, didn't so much as glance at me or Joe.

Joe noticed my confusion and smiled. Still looking at me he raised his voice and said, "Hey! Moira! Were you in there peeping on my boy in the bathroom? We've talked about this! Doing it to the entire staff is one thing, but guests and friends of mine is taking it too far!"

He giggled and looked over at her. She barely acknowledged him, looking up briefly to give him a fake smile as if to say 'very funny!', and went back to putting bottles in the cooler. He laughed and motioned me over to the bar for a seat.

"The booze closet is inside the men's room, she must have been back there already when you walked in. But if she touched you, this is a safe place for you to tell me!" He cracked himself up for about a minute and got back into owner mode. He started telling me about the structure of their service. "You saw the menu...three courses for $45, and we have two seatings. One at 6pm and one at 8:30. We open at 5:30. Official closing time is 11:00, but if people are buying drinks I'll keep it open past that. We get some decent bar business early and late, first responder types, friends of mine, definitely industry people. I wouldn't call this a drinking destination, but we will go through some beers and shots on a good night."

"Weekends much busier? You have to staff up for that?" I asked.

"It's very rare that we are just slammed...we never over-book, so we'll take walk-ins but we don't have that many. Three servers, busser slash runner, host slash manager and bartender has been a solid equation. Two bartenders on the weekend. Everyone can run food or step in when needed. We keep it professional but not formal. The two seatings makes timing easier without making it full-on banquet service, and with the late start to the second one the customers aren't rushed and it can buy the kitchen some time during and between seatings. Eighty to ninety covers is us running full steam, we've done over a hundred a couple of times. Just depends on how the butts in seats break down for the individual reservations. During the week it's lower, around sixty covers on average. No nightly specials, but I have a process where about a week before the new menu I'll start replacing items on the current one."

"You write the whole menu? Develop it with your cooks?" For someone who wasn't, as he claimed, a 'real chef', Joe had what sounded like a very scaleable and sturdy process for running his place.

"For our food we don't need much in the way of a test kitchen...a lot of the time it's a conversation in the kitchen during prep or after service that inadvertently ends up on the menu. If one of my guys has a brainstorm or something specific we haven't done before I'm never going to shoot them down. It may or may not make the menu, or it will be on in some other form, and everyone has input when we're dialing in the recipes and extrapolating everything out batch and prep-wise. The hot fried chicken is a good example...one of my cooks was talking about hot wings as an appetizer, which I wasn't too keen on. You either have to go straight traditional which I didn't want, or there's some hellish shitty prep on a metric ton of wings every day...like those lollipops. Anyway, Cesar and I have both messed around with different fried chicken recipes, so the fried boneless thighs came out of that and dunking them in hot sauce was a no-brainer. I'm not pretending this is fine dining, to my staff or my guests. It's more supper than dinner, if that makes any sense."

"Your servers make out okay?" I asked.

"Tips you mean? That's steady, no issues. People who are straight middle-class seem to be pretty generous. In the big picture of fine dining, a $45 meal is a joke. Where I'm from, that's a chunk. Especially if you're bringing your family out. Hundreds of dollars."

"Oh, absolutely, you and I are both rich people now when you think about how we grew up." Finally a solid member of the middle-class, the amount I spend on dining is something I think about often. When you get to a point where you can choose between "nice" and "cheap" meals on a date night, and the burgers or tacos you consider cheap are still an out of reach luxury for many, you have to be careful not to lose perspective. It makes you respect the fact that many of your celebration dinners as a kid were a bigger sacrifice than your parents let on.

"True. True," he said. "We've got good diners in this town. People who enjoy the time together instead of hit and run Applebee's shit. Plus, last year our average check was north of $75. That's liquor. I can't remember if I mentioned, but we move some booze. A lot of wine. And I try not to gouge the shit out of people who are looking for a nice bottle with their meal. The mark-up is a learning curve for people who don't order a lot of it in restaurants, so I keep it as transparent as possible. I'd be curious to talk to some of your Beard winners and ask about how it all works on that level of dining. Oh, and I have a five-dollar corkage fee...people appreciate that. We're the definition of a special occasion place, a very weird one, so by all means I'm going to let them bring wine. No cakes or desserts though. That's a hard rule."

"I'm very weird about who I will eat with," I told him, "people are either already close friends of mine, or vetted by close friends. I'm not too good for them, but I eat where I'm a regular and my time there is special to me...if you're a bad tipper, someone who will bitch and try to rewrite the menu, or if I get even a whiff of 'Jerry will get us the hookup', you're on my banned list. Forever. I have zero, absolute zero, obligation to spend time with people if I don't click with them."

"Now one thing that pisses me off," Joe said, "and we don't see it here too often, but I get sucked into online arguments about these dicks. It's people who will buy a bunch of wine or booze, or one really expensive bottle of wine, and then subtract it from the total before they tip."

"Oh my god," I said, "that is pariah-level behavior, I would never share my table with them."

"It's control, has nothing to do with the money. If you can buy it, you can tip on it. Period. These assholes...'Well, all they did was open a bottle, why do they deserve a huge tip on that?' I don't know prick, maybe because you're a high roller and it's the right thing? I'm serious, I might come out of the kitchen over that, without exception you're a complete piece of shit and your parents were complete pieces of shit if you do that. Your kids are probably on their way to being pieces of shit too. Fuck you. I don't need your business."

"Well the big thing now is whether or not tipping is still a relevant custom...so there's that." I brought that up to get Joe's input as a Midwestern chef.

"No disrespect to a hospitality pioneer, but thanks Mr. Billionaire for giving already shitty tippers who have no clue how the industry works a reason to complain even more." He rolled his eyes and continued. "I totally get the argument, and in a perfect world where people are willing to pay what food and overhead costs, that would be optimum. But people like the wine assholes use tipping as a carrot and stick, so they'll immediately bitch that servers won't care anymore if you can't reward or punish them. Worse service for more expensive food. You can't win. Tipping isn't going anywhere."

"Oh, I know. Morons. Mr. Pink from *Reservoir Dogs*. I've never met anyone worth knowing who has a detailed tipping strategy," I added.

"Nothing will change anytime soon. Just another way for people with no skin in the game to feel like they know something." Joe shifted on his bar seat, laughed and said, "You know, the people who have a chef's jacket at home! They wear them when having a dinner party, and always forget a key ingredient so they can wear it into Whole Foods!"

I'd met my share of those folks through the years. "Ha! Got a six top! At my house! Gotta bang out these scallops! CORNER! Order fire! All the jargon!"

"No shit...TV has fucking ruined people." He sighed and continued talking. "Everybody has their pet peeves. Bad tippers are a big one for me. And people who ask their server's name immediately after they're seated. That has always struck me like a creepy power play. 'I'm just being polite!' Yeah, bullshit. It's condescending as shit, 'Hello my lesser! I am your friend and a human person just like you! My grandmother who did this back in the slave days told me this was polite! You're still on the hook for those iced tea refills though!'"

"I've only run into that when I've happened to be out with co-workers, which is rare. Always a dude who has a copy of a book like 'Who Moved My Cheese?' at his desk, or sends emails about effective habits for managers. Talks to himself in the mirror. Seeks reassurance from his buddies...'Yeah bro, you really connected with that stripper last night, it was way more than you giving her all of your money!'"

He laughed and stood up from his seat. "I swear to god, one of these days one of them is going to slip up and answer back, 'Well nice to meet you Michelle! That's also the name of the girl I have chained in my basement…do you like Huey Lewis?"

It was closing in on 3:00, two-and-a-half hours before the doors opened. While we were talking, a blonde girl in a long-sleeved white blouse and black skirt had arrived and started work at the host station. I assumed it was his other longtime employee Tina. Between our venting, I looked over and she smiled big and waved. I smiled back. When we finished our conversation, Joe walked over to say something to her, and then went back into the kitchen. She had the computer up and it looked like she was checking reservations against some paperwork on the desk. Within about a minute, she picked up the phone…"Hello, this is Tina calling from The Five to confirm your reservation…" and on it went as I sat there in the relative quiet. Any time she would catch my eye she would smile. It was cute and a hilarious counterpoint to what was going on ten feet away from her. Moira never stopped what she was doing while I talked to Joe. She kept working without a sound or acknowledgment of anyone else in the room. Then suddenly she grabbed a five-gallon

clear plastic bucket and disappeared into the kitchen.
Within a couple of minutes she was back with a haul of ice
from the basement. She repeated that a few times, filling
the well behind the bar and the one in the server station at
the end closest to the bathroom. From somewhere in the
building either the furnace or air conditioner kicked on.
What little ambient light made it into The Five intensified
from the west windows as the sun shifted downward. A
few minutes passed and Joe appeared from the kitchen. He
had a metal strongbox in his hand, which he delivered to
Tina. He started to introduce her to me until he realized
she was talking to a guest on the phone.

Joe walked over to the bar and stood between
Moira and myself. He put his hands on the edge of the bar
and did a couple of what I would describe as shallow
pushups as he would first look at me, then at her, then me,
then her. In my experience as a Midwestern shit-talker, his
behavior signaled some level of jokery was about to
commence.

"Moira!" It began. "Did you tell my friend Jerry
here all about your list of specialty cocktails? Jerry, did she
just yap away the whole time I was gone? I think Jerry here
knows quite a bit about mixology, Moira. You should
seriously talk to him, lots of good stuff is happening in

Kansas City, get some feedback on your drinks!"

She ignored him completely, looked at me and asked, "Can I get you anything to drink?"

She had a pronounced but not a movie villain level of a Russian accent. I told her I was fine, and looking at me Joe said, "OH! Did you see that? Not even so much as a glance! She's focused though. I'll give her that. Moira is the most-focused employee we've ever had. Her focus is so strong that she hasn't been able to write the drink menu I asked for. When was that? Two years ago?"

Still only speaking to me she said, "Chef asked me to write a drink menu. It's a stupid idea. That's for college kids. No college kids here. No drink menu. People here don't drink like children."

Joe made a production out of wiping away a fake tear. "Jerry...Moira here and Tina have been with us since my parents were alive. And I don't think I have ever experienced such an emotional moment as this." He drew it out for effect, "This is the first time that my dear friend Moira here has called me the C-word. She loves me! You *love* me, don't you?"

The faintest of a faint, tiny twitch of the

beginning of a smile flashed at the corner of Moira's mouth and was gone. She did not respond.

"Moira and I are basically an arranged marriage. A very bad one," he said. "But she loves me. Not enough for me to ever get a drink menu, but she loves me. Moira, I was about to tell Jerry here about our guest who made the paper!"

Without looking up she muttered, "THAT piece of shit..."

Moira finished polishing some wine glasses, grabbed some lemons and limes that were under the liquor shelves behind her and began cutting them. She piled them neatly into a condiment holder as she went. No other employees had arrived for work yet. Tina had finished confirming upcoming reservations, and took the strongbox Joe brought her and walked back to the server station. She turned on the point of sale terminal and changed the paper in the credit card machine. Then she opened the cash drawer and filled it with money from the metal box.

Joe and I were still sitting at the bar. He was situated between me and Tina. She was finishing some kind of data entry in the computer before picking up the box and taking it into the kitchen. I assumed there was an office downstairs I hadn't seen. He pointed with his thumb and told me, "Tina is awesome. She has been here since she was a teenager waiting tables at Juric's. Our families go way back. She's in my OG Hall of Fame along with Cesar and Moira. Super nice, but very, very chatty. I love her, but there is a very fine line between saying hello to her and the rest of your day disappearing once she starts talking. And she cries easily...so basically she is the absolute OPPOSITE OF MOIRA!" He raised his voice, but it fell on deaf ears. Apparently not yet satisfied, he yelled, "TINA! Come back in here!", and then he looked at me and said, "Watch this!"

She walked back into the bar looking a little bewildered. "What's up, Chef?" She had a very slight Southern accent, or maybe just a more pronounced Midwestern one.

Joe leaned towards her, looking very serious with his fists clenched on his knees. He started to sing in a low, croaking voice. "God is in…his holy temple…God is in…his HOLY TEMPLE!"

Tina backed away with her hands up as if she were surrendering and shook them. "STOP! I HATE that!"

He did not stop. "You're all gonna DIE in there!"

"I'm serious Joe, I get nightmares about that shit! I hate it!" She was frustrated, I could see it turning into tears if he kept going.

"I'm smart," Joe spoke softly, "and I'm your friend, and I know…what you are thinking."

"Oh my GOD!" She gave him a look of total aggravation and disappeared back into the kitchen.

He sat there laughing and looking at me. "That old man from *Poltergeist*…totally freaks her out. I'll be honest. I'm not the best guy to confide in if you're drunk and talking about what really scares you." Then once again he called her, "TINA! Seriously, come on back in here!"

She may have been pausing for effect, but after half a minute she walked back in. "What, Joe?"

"How has your day been so far, Tina?" He deadpanned.

"Just fine Joe, how about your day?" She returned it in kind.

He nodded his head and in a serious tone he said, "Not bad. Not bad. This is Jerry, my friend from Kansas

City I've been telling you about."

She walked over to me to shake my hand, smiled and said, "It is a pleasure to meet you, Jerry! Is Joe being nice to you? He's not very good at introductions."

"Nice to meet you too, yeah he's been great. I really like your restaurant. Joe has told me a little about you guys, some good things."

"Oh really?" She gave Joe a smile, but less thank you and more kiss my ass. She definitely took theatre in high school.

Joe stuck with the serious tone. "Tina, I told Jerry about the soup."

"The soup?"

"Yeah, that day Cesar called all of you guys to come in and I'd made all of that soup. I told Jerry the whole story."

She stared at him for a few moments, no expression on her face. "I get what you're doing here. Not today, smartass. Jerry! Instead of crying in front of you like Joe is expecting, I'm going to get back to work, but I'm very happy you're here and even though he is awful I'm glad he gets to tell you about our restaurant."

She gave Joe a final perturbed look and went back through the kitchen door. He just chuckled, celebrating only half of a victory since she did not cry. I hoped to get some time around Cesar as well, if not on that trip then one in the near future. With the extreme personality differences between Moira and Tina, I had no idea what to expect from him. Almost everything I was seeing between Joe and his team was pure ball-busting, but that's how it goes with crews who spend that much time together. There was obviously a deep love shared between them, but they were doing an awesome job putting on a show for company. Except for Moira. I had a strong suspicion her personality did not deviate far from exactly what Joe described.

"So your three OG's are it for your long-term staff?" I asked.

"Yeah, these three go back to the original restaurant. My server Paula was on staff when it was both of us brothers running the place. Everyone else is less than year. Two servers and a dishwasher are *brand* new...so nobody can fall in love yet."

"What do you mean?"

"Don't get too attached...they can just disappear. I always pretend I don't even learn anyone's name until they're here at least six months. Anyway...the cop. I'm sorry, I get sidetracked and I know you came out here for specific stuff. But you're not much help either. You're as full of shit as I am," he said.

"I know, I would have just talked food and old neighborhood restaurants all day. But no worries, I'll be back out here regardless." I always joked about how I was terrible at writing if I had rules and a timeline, but it was becoming a reality for me. I was having a good time and I kept forgetting why I came out in the first place.

"WELL, the backstory on that first newspaper article, which got us quite a bump in business I might add, goes back to before The Five was the cultural juggernaut it is today..." He pursed his lips and shook his head dismissively at that statement. Joe said, "It was still just a friends and family situation that started with that family I mentioned who lost their house, et cetera. It was very word-of-mouth for that aspect of the place, with the majority of our business being people off the street and Juric's regulars who were checking out the new restaurant. We got a booking from a teenage girl whose dad was a cop friend of another cop my family has known for a long time. Table for four, there was nothing that indicated it was anything other than a normal dinner reservation. But apparently Little Miss Movie of the Week had the whole thing planned out based on whatever intel she'd gotten from who the hell knows. So they show up, it's her and her parents and some kid who is apparently her boyfriend."

"Oh hell," I said, "this could go a lot of directions. Were they white and he was black?"

"Ha! No, no, but the *Guess Who's Coming to Dinner* angle is imaginative. I like that. No, she was there to announce her pregnancy."

"Well, the paper kind of gave away the ending. How long did it take for the shit to hit the fan?" I asked.

"Way faster than you would expect! They did not make it through the soup and salad course before she spilled it, and the reaction was immediate."

"Were there a lot of other people in here?" I was fascinated.

"I don't know if the girl was thinking a bigger crowd would keep her dad from going fucking Godzilla on the kid, so yes, it was Saturday night and it was a full house," he answered.

"Oh my god, Joe, I feel bad for your staff having to deal with that, but holy shit that would have been something to see."

He looked at me with that same pursed lip look he had earlier, but this time was nodding his head. "Yes. It was absolutely something to see. We didn't know the full story until later, because from what my servers told me the first sign of a possible issue was when the guy stood up and fucking dragged the kid *across* the table by the shirt collar and proceeded to slap the dogshit out of him. Doesn't say a single word, just collars him and starts hitting. What does the mastermind of this dinner do? She immediately runs to the bathroom and locks the door, with her mother giving chase. The first thing I hear to make me aware I've got fucking Hell in a Cell popping off in my dining room is a chorus of servers and some regulars screaming "JOE!" It's unsettling to hear your name like that during service when you're the Chef, so I ran out of the kitchen and the first thing I see is some lady pounding on the bathroom door...of course they picked the one right by the dining room instead of the bar...and she's yelling at her daughter to come out, the daughter is screaming back at her. I get to the entrance to the dining room, and there he is slapping the kid who could very well be his future son-in-law! A little awkward, right? And I mean fucking bitch slapping...reaching back to fucking Kansas City and open palm whomping at that boy. It hurt to look at it, I thought he would be deaf at a minimum after that."

"Jesus Christ! Nobody was doing anything?"

"I guess Good Samaritan night was Friday night, because they are all glued to their seats in shock watching it. My staff all know I'd fire them for putting themselves in danger. And I get it, it happened fast plus everything about the guy screamed 'cop'...including a pistol down his back you could see when his shirt popped up during the beat-down. It wasn't normal to be happening in my restaurant, but breaking that shit up wouldn't be my first rodeo. In between smacks I just stepped in between the kid and that pimp hand and yelled, 'THIS IS OVER!' He snaps out of it, drops the kid onto what would have been perfectly lovely starters to their meal, and storms out the front door."

"That is just insane," I said. "Way to go Topeka!"

He snapped his fingers to indicate he remembered something. "Oh! I take it back, my guests didn't sit idly by as it went down. At least ten of them must have dialed 911 on their cell phones saying someone was being killed, because three minutes after I broke it up every cop car in the state of Kansas was in front of the building. *That* is what finally got the instigator out of the bathroom, and she and her mother bailed too."

"What about the kid?" I asked.

"He was a little fucked up. I sent him back into the kitchen with a couple of my servers to check him out and see if he needed an ambulance, and if not to just help him get cleaned up a little. A few cops came in to talk to him. I didn't hear what was said, but they were all gone in about ten minutes. I sat him at the bar, gave him some beers. I figured if nobody was going to jail for beating his ass, nobody was going to ding me for serving a minor. I drove him home later that night. I was mainly hoping I wouldn't somehow be found liable and get sued over the incident...crazier shit has happened."

"Did you finish service?"

"Yes!" He said it proudly. "When the cops all left, I did a little song and dance to help smooth things over and gave away a lot of liquor. There was a crazy energy, like adrenaline. Everybody was probably thrilled to have a story to tell."

"What about the arrest?" I asked.

"Interesting postscript there. Whipping boy's dad is a judge, so that shit did not fly. I think the guy got some unpaid administrative leave and there had to be some kind of pain and duress settlement I'm sure. They perp walked his ass though, on TV and everything after they arrested him at his home. I don't know how it would have ended if the kid's dad wasn't a judge, but with social media and all that it's not like when me and you were kids..."

Oh yeah," I said, "we would have taken the ass whipping and that would be that...knocking up a cop's daughter...may have ended up in the caves out in Wolcott."

Joe laughed and said, "I was thinking about driving by the house sometime to check and see how the grandbaby is doing!"

That literally made me laugh out loud, and I had to add, "Can I offer you this quart of my famous Kansas City Steak Soup to help you all through this trying time?"

That sent Joe into a laughing and coughing fit for a minute. "Ohhhh shit, so yeah, that incident got us some unintended advertisement. Could have gone either way though. Instead of bad news you bring in someone needing a beat-down. We'd make it the redneck version of that Medieval Times place. My parents would have been so proud...sister fuckers and cuckolds sprawled out all over their floor."

By that time in the afternoon, Tina and Moira had either gone outside or downstairs. They were nowhere to be seen. A young man and woman walked in quietly while we were talking and went to a closet between the bathroom and kitchen door to retrieve piles of linens. Then they went into the kitchen and returned a couple of minutes later with grey plastic bins of silverware. I needed to get up and stretch for a minute and Joe stepped outside for a quick smoke. I went back and took a seat at the bar. The interaction between Joe and his staff reminded me what a close, and to some extent closed, culture the service industry can be. As an outsider, you can get a glimpse like I did with Cesar yelling at a new cook or Joe pressing Tina's buttons. But you have to hang around a while and really get to know people before you gain a level of trust that goes beyond it.

A simple, but significant, moment that always comes to mind was at my favorite restaurant during employee lineup right before service. I was sitting at the chef's counter while the cooks were going over that night's specials with the servers. Every dish went from person to person, everyone taking a bite of each special and passing it along. As they moved down the row, I became the last stop for each of the dishes. It may have looked like a simple courtesy, but it was also a test I didn't recognize at first. Each dish was on its own plate, but everyone shared the same fork or spoon as the food came around. I realized I was getting eyeballed but at first I thought it was to see if I approved of the dish. And though I'm sure people were happy if I liked the food, it was more about "Is he going to eat from the community spoon?" I didn't even think about it, I'm way beyond worrying about sharing silverware. I don't expect it to make sense to most people, but it's those little details that help you understand the community in an organic way.

Joe was back within two minutes and sat down next to me at the bar. One basic factor in the restaurant's protocol had come to mind a couple of times that day, but I finally remembered to ask. "Joe, big question here…I understand how the theme or legend, however it should be labeled, got started. And now I'm beginning to understand what made the concept take off, but how does it work? Do people just make reservations? Are there rules? Do you ask people any questions? Is there a percentage of your reservations that are just folks wanting to eat your food?"

"*That* is a smart question," Joe said. "Because I know it sounded insane enough to bring you out here. But yes, people just make reservations, and no there are no rules or any kind of screening other than the person making the reservation has to be at least 21. And that is only because of the Teen Mom incident."

"Validating a minimum age makes sense." I said.

"Can you imagine if this was the default place for that shit?" he asked. "All teen pregnancy related...are they keeping it? Are they having an abortion? What do the parents have to say? Jesus Christ, I'd have to build twenty more bathrooms so they could all scream at each other through the doors."

"That would be your whole gig, they'd come from all over!"

"No shit, if I were just wanting to make a buck on it I'd host Sunday high teas just for them or something. Everybody dress up in their Easter finest and come fucking weep. No dads!" he added.

"So 21 and over..."

"Yes. We haven't had anything else pop off like that, no weird agendas ending in violence anyway. I think we have enough notoriety at this point that nobody is a big enough dumbass to ask their wife or husband- 'Hey honey want to have dinner at The Five? What? Oh, no reason…' and then tell them the marriage is over. I guess it could happen, maybe it has happened, but my people are very sensitive to sudden spikes in drama, and are good about checking in with me during service if I'm too busy to make it out there."

"So just how many people, what date and what time? Nothing about the occasion?" I asked.

"Nope, that's it. Believe me, nine times out of ten people are more than willing to share the information all on their own. If something really sticks out, Tina or whomever is taking the res might mention it to me later, but I think for most people it's part of their process if they're grieving or whatever is going on. And that's cool, there's no judgment as far as that goes unless someone is angling for VIP treatment based on their situation."

"People do that?" With all of the blind entitlement I'd witnessed over the years, I still couldn't comprehend that type of customer.

"Oh yeah! I know you're not new to the shit people will pull to get any tiny crumb! If someone is a shameless piece of shit, grief or pain isn't going to change that. They'll usually want to talk to me directly and will assume I'm going to say 'Dead MOTHER? Oh yes! You are the winner! Champagne and the best table in the house!' or afraid I'll say 'Skin cancer? Let me look at the reservation book...oh no, fuck off, we've got a stage 4 pancreatic coming in that night with their whole family. Can I take your number? If they don't bring hospice workers with them I MIGHT be able to squeeze you in!' Shit doesn't work that way. I don't require a story to eat here. Bring your appetite and your money, that's it."

"What brings people in? Anything stand out more than everything else?" I asked.

"Obviously, there is a fair share of deaths, divorce aftermath, job losses, standard stuff. But you know the number one thing? And I mean, no exaggeration, the thing that keeps our doors open? You won't fucking believe it, but then it will make complete sense..."

"What is it?" I hadn't even tried thinking beyond the obvious yet.

"Pets, bro." He cocked his head back and smirked

like he was Sherlock Holmes cracking a case. "Dead pets. As God is my witness, the biggest tabs we ring for the biggest parties are all one hundred percent animal-related! Entire families. Young children through grandparents. Dead pets, man. White people with enough money to book an eight-top on a random Wednesday take that shit seriously. I don't want to sound like I'm making fun, I get it, and everyone has their own threshold and process. I am grateful for them, they're my bread and butter. I've lost pets, but I've lost way more people. It's not the same thing."

"Holy hell, you're right. It makes sense. But no, not the same thing. I guess it would be cool to live in that bubble. But good for you though, man! Score!"

"No shit! Dead pet lottery!" Joe clapped his hands once and did a double thumbs-up. "I'll think of a hundred examples once you leave, but the big things that pop to mind when people book are people moving away, deployments, death anniversaries and birthdays...people headed to jail, actually."

"Anybody we know?" I joked.

"You'd think! Oh, the best bookings, we have only had a couple but I hope they catch on, is someone heading to rehab the next day. Monster-sized tickets, and they are fun as hell. You want to drink with the owner after hours? Be headed to rehab! Awesome parties."

"That sounds perfect! I'll let my sober friends know where to head between falling off the wagon and heading back to rehab in Atchison!"

He reached over and we shook on it. "I joke around, but this place saved me. I sound jaded, and I am jaded, but that doesn't mean I don't appreciate what I've got. I do a lot of comps. A lot of referrals from family and friends. Anyone just wanting a good meal can come here, there is no sorrow requirement. We make very good food. But some people need it, man. People who don't have the soundness of mind to call for a reservation, but they need to belong someplace for a few hours, and they need to eat. I'll just leave it at that. Some people are so grateful and so good it makes you cry."

Joe was quiet for a bit, looking down at the bar, working something out in his head and then looking back up at me. "This place is limbo, you know? You stop in here and you may be headed to heaven, or you may be headed to hell afterwards. But this is a safe place for a while. Things will get much better, or they will get worse, but I'm going to feed you good food that speaks to me. And I've been both directions. So, you can trust me with that."

Another server had arrived; a young lady who immediately began going from table to table, rocking them side-to-side to gauge how much wobble each one had. For the worst offenders, she pulled something out of her pocket and knelt down to place it under a leg before retesting to make sure the table placement was firm. She was straightening all of the dining room chairs as she went. At the same time, the other two servers were at a corner table pulling sets of silverware from the bins, polishing the pieces and rolling them neatly into white linen napkins. Tina stood at the server station getting a fresh pot of coffee brewing. Joe received a text on his phone and headed back into the kitchen.

He had a self-deprecating nature that I appreciated, but he was a worker...taking off this much time during the day to chat and share his story was a luxury for him. I was honored to be the person who got this story, even though I had no idea what I was going to do with it. He was under no obligation to take that risk, and if everything he was telling me was true it wasn't like he needed any advertisement to get butts in seats. I paced the bar for a little while until Joe returned.

"Fucking dishwasher just called in... maybe Burt Reynolds snuck in here when I wasn't looking and wanted to see his dick for a movie." He announced from the kitchen door on his way back into the bar.

"The new one?'

"Yeah, that was him...*was* him! This is why I tell my people not to fall in love. Two strikes and you're out. Anyway, double shifts are the theme today, my morning guy is going to stay for service."

Tina was finishing up at the server station and asked, "Joe, you want me to go through applications later so we can get someone new in here quick? We've got at least ten, none are brand new but new enough to give it a shot. Cesar knows a couple of them already, I know that for sure."

"Yes! Please!" He clapped his hands for emphasis, and then he laughed. "Jerry, you're getting some serious bonus action here! You want to go outside and go over some applications with me? Help me find a new dishwasher?"

"Yeah, Joe, sure..." I was kind of surprised he

wanted to do that, "I'll do whatever you need. You want me to read through some?"

"No, you dumbass!" He and Tina both laughed. "I'm fucking with you. I mean, feel free but you'd probably rather hear about my dad's drunk war buddies."

Some light hazing is another way to know you're beginning to make real friends.

.

-6-

The servers were all at work putting the finishing touches on the dining room, and the smells and sounds coming from the kitchen indicated everything was in full swing. The small tables in the bar were outfitted with a faceted crystal tea light holder and a small red ceramic vase with a few neatly arranged dried flowers. In the dining room, white tablecloths were being draped on each of the tables, followed by the same candles and vases as in the bar. Silverware, wine and water glasses, and plain white bread plates followed. A tray filled with sugar caddies and salt and pepper shakers was retrieved from the station by the pass, and the server who had arrived last began wiping down each of the shakers. I couldn't remember the last time I'd seen salt and pepper shakers on the tables in a higher-end restaurant.

Joe was about to lead me out the front door, and stopped to ask, "You hanging out for service?"

"Sure, I'd love to have dinner. I can sit at the bar or wherever if you're full up."

"Nah, fuck that." He said. "Tina must be downstairs grabbing job applications...Paula! Come here for a sec!" He called to the girl who was busy cleaning the shakers, and she came over.

"What's up, Chef?" she asked, smiling and looking back and forth between Joe and me.

"Paula, this is my old friend Jerry. He's been spending the day with me to learn about the restaurant, and he's going to be having dinner with us...check with Tina and see if you can put him in your section when we open."

"Will do!" she said, "Nice to meet you, see you in a bit!" And she went right back to what she was doing.

Joe stepped back over to the bar to collect his beers and motioned his head toward the door. I followed close behind, back towards the picnic table. One of the cooks was finishing a cigarette and going back inside as we came around the corner.

"Paula is super cool," Joe turned to tell me as we walked past the parking lot, "she's my veteran server, finishing up college so I don't know how long she'll be here. I'm glad for her, but it sucks, people love her. She's from Pentecostal royalty here in town, it's a whole story. She's working in a place that serves alcohol now, so to her family I'm basically Satan. She'll take care of you, feel free to get her input on the place. Or anyone's really, if you get the chance. We'll blow you up good tonight. Glad you're staying to eat."

"Oh, I know what being Satan feels like!" I told him, making a mental note to swap stories the next time I visited.

He went back to the exact same spot at the picnic table as before, facing out toward the parking lot so that he could lean back on the table. I sat at the end of the bench beside him. He took a long pull from his Miller High Life, lit his cigarette, took a deep drag and sat there for a minute staring far off towards the east.

"You know," he said, "the one thing I'm grateful for as far as the paper doing that big article is that now we never get anyone asking if The Five has anything to do with that stupid fucking Fox News show. Sure, look where we are, I could have played that up and we'd be full every night with old people who keep their TV volume maxed out with that shit. People with maybe two election cycles left in them. Death's waiting room. We didn't get it *that* often, but often enough to be annoying. So I'm happy that stopped. And any advertisement is good."

"Unless it's a murder, obviously," I said.

"Obviously! But Jerry, be totally honest...what did you feel or think about The Five being named after my dad and his army buddies?"

"What is there to think? Your late father fought in Vietnam and built this restaurant. It needs no validation. If you want to be callous about it, it is a golden business move, it's bullet-proof."

He sighed and nodded his head, his gaze never moving from some point on the horizon. "And THAT is why I wish it was not complete bullshit."

"You've alluded to it a couple of times, but I didn't want to ask...it's your story."

"Well, my dad and his friends were all in the war, which is absolutely accurate. He never shared many details, but they saw real shit. There should be more than five of them, I'll say that much. These are men I've known my whole life, I know when we originally moved to Topeka one factor was getting the whole gang back together. My brother Tom and I were named after two of them, so they're family. Multiply all of that times similar old school immigrant backgrounds, and it's not only something you could name your restaurant for, fucking Scorsese could make a script out of it."

I agreed. "It's rock solid, Joe."

"I am telling you this in order to emphasize the fact that the family bond is permanent. We call them all Uncle. For all I know one of them saved my father's life. When he died, they were ready to scrub toilets or invest money to keep these doors open. When Tom died it was a given that they would take care of every detail that was needed. I am framing it for you this way on purpose, to emphasize the depth of our connection with these men, one whose name I carry, so that you know exactly what it means for me to say...I would take a bat to the back of that motherfucker's head and work my way down the line, drop all four of them in a fucking ditch, have a nice meal and then sleep like a baby."

That was such a shock it was hard to know how to react. Even though Joe had dropped ample hints that not everything was as it seemed with his dad's buddies, it was a face full of cold water to hear him talk like that. We weren't close to the greatest kids growing up, but respect for elders and especially veterans was hardwired into us as much as religious guilt. I know he said it to make a point and get a reaction, but the most I had for him was a blank stare and, "Damn, Joe. Goddamn."

He had broken out of his far-off gaze and was watching my face as he dropped that bomb. He looked genuinely angry, his jaw tight and fists clenched, like a man who had honestly contemplated murder. But as soon as it left his mouth, his body relaxed like the act of expelling the words relieved him of a huge weight he'd been carrying. A controlled exhale punctuated the physical change, steady like he was holding a breathalyzer between his lips. He smirked and it could have been out of resignation or simple pride in leaving me close to speechless. "I can't do that. But every time I see those grinning dipshits it comes to mind. I don't know if they were bored, if it was a conspiracy, or just some unfortunate drunken timing on their part, but they fucked us. Joe...that's Uncle Joe, is the ringleader with my dad gone, so he'd have to die first."

"Joe, all I can say is that you have a gift for painting one hell of a picture." It was going to take me a long time to mentally unpack everything he was telling me. The goal of writing some canned article was long gone. I was worried about how to break that to Joe, since it was the reason I made the trip and why he took a day off to talk with me. I would have to choose one piece of the story to write about, and that would never work. I had no idea how much Joe was still going to tell me, and zero clue how to frame what I knew so far. He was finally beginning to divulge how his restaurant got its name, and the origin was sounding like an elaborate prank at best or a major betrayal at worst. That's not how restaurants get their names. And if one did get its name that way, you would never read about it in an electronic food and beverage periodical.

Before he began his explanation, he put his hands behind his head and locked his fingers in the same way you do right after the cop tells you to first step out of the car. He stared ahead and didn't smile so much as bare his teeth like he was looking in a mirror to see if any food was stuck. He put his hands back down and tilted his head back as he started working through the series of events.

"I got a call from the newspaper not long after the cop got arrested, but it wasn't about that incident in particular," Joe said. "I think our lack of internet presence, plus that arrest, plus whatever else the reporter had heard just had them curious to find out about the restaurant in general. We talked a while and I gave them the majority of what you read...the overall history, family information, all of that. They thought the story would be a good human interest fit for them, and I was pumped to get the free press. The lady I spoke with told me she'd like to stop by one evening with their photographer to get some pictures for the story. Simple enough, I'm always here, and I told her earlier was better than later but stopping by during service was fine whenever she had time."

He took the last gulp from one beer and a sip from the next. I hadn't kept a count of how many he'd had, but if he was anything like most of the guys I grew up with it would take a whole lot more of them to affect him any more than the same number of sodas. He continued, "So of course she stopped in when the doors opened on the one night I'd be late for service. And the first person she met was Uncle Joe, and whichever of the other bastards he was with revving up for a bender."

"Are they in here a lot?" I asked.

"Yes! Oh fuck yes! There's no getting rid of them! I mean, maybe if I ever gave them a tab for all the shit beer they suck down it would scare them off! But yeah, this is their Croatian and Polish version of the Ravenite goddamn Social Club or something. You'll see at least two of them at the start of service, or they'll be here at closing...always two or more, never one. Like teenage girls, but with those black and gold U.S. Veteran trucker caps."

Joe stared far out past the parking lot again, smiled and laughed silently. "I'll give him credit. If it's something he came up with on the fly, it was pretty genius. Anyway, the reporter walks in and asks for me, finds out I'm not here and falls in with the drunk uncle greeting committee. They're great at playing the charming old man role, double that when they saw the fancy camera...immigrant stories, war stories, and I guarantee most of what they talked about wasn't bullshit. They are characters, but they come by it honestly."

"But the one thing they *did* bullshit..." I started and Joe finished my thought.

"THE FIVE! They stole the name of my fucking restaurant! Never once in my entire life with them did we *ever* discuss anything related to my dad and the war. But after a couple of beers with a stranger from the newspaper it's all, 'ooohhhh we're soooooo honored to have served and now to have our best friend and service recognized by his sons.' Never fucking happened! I don't know if it was some shit they dreamed up after we opened the place, or if they'd already been telling people around town or what."

"Shit, Joe," I said, "that's one hell of an over-step,

but is there a chance they were trying to do a good thing maybe? For your dad's memory or something?"

"No! I know them. I know their tells. The shit-eating grin that Uncle Joe gets on his face when he's pulled some con is something I've known my whole life. To him he was telling a bullshit story to some lady who showed interest, and my best guess is he had no idea it would actually see the light of day. That stupid grin is the same one he had when they finally got the balls to start coming back in here. They all think it's funny as shit."

"They disappeared? When did you find out what happened?" I asked.

"I saw it when everyone else did. When it was in the paper. I got a follow-up email from the reporter the morning after her visit telling me she stopped in and got some photos, talked to some regulars, but nothing about old men giving her the scoop on the name of the place. They are convincing, that's what they do! And like I mentioned, most of what they said was probably the truth. I didn't see or hear from them for over a week once the article came out, and for them that's the equivalent of a year of being away from their little club. That's another reason the whole thing was bullshit, they knew they fucked up and hid."

"Did you ever follow up with the reporter when it came out?" It sounded to me like an extreme omission for a reporter to skip that specific detail when following up with the owner.

"No. How would you approach that? Hey wait! I have a very boring and shitty story to tell you about the name! You need to retract the American success story immigrant war hero memorial thing! The truth is way shittier! Let's go with that! See what I mean? Those bastards made up a great story. I still have days when I want to drop their bodies in my dumpster, but it's a goddamn great story."

I agreed. "Honestly, it's such a great story that it may not even need to be true. Shit, your Uncle Joe could just say that YOU are the liar if the truth ever came out...combat veteran wins, no question."

"Absolutely! I didn't even talk to my staff about it. Everyone was pumped to see the place in the paper, but nobody knows the real story behind the name, or at least they act like they don't for my sake. So before you ask, yes, I will tell you. You're the first to get the story, and you can do whatever you want with it."

I was genuinely honored, but at the same time had to be honest about where I was at with his story. "I'm excited to hear about it Joe, and I don't want you to get the wrong idea when I say this, but I don't know what to do with it. All of this, actually. It's a fantastic story, I just don't want to shrink it down to a few thousand words and give it to someone to chop up and put in their online magazine. If I take your story and it gets wedged in between an ad for some local soccer mom jewelry store and an article for the Best French Fries in Kansas City, I'm going to feel like an asshole. I'd still do it if you really wanted it, but it's too good to end up as a timewaster story for people to read at work."

He was quiet for a few seconds and then told me, "The rest of my team will probably be bummed, but I get it. I honestly don't care, we have customers and the place is running pretty well. We've never had to depend on advertising. But my people, some of them have gone through the same shit that I have. They lost my family too. I know Moira and Tina worry about me too much to ever bring up anything they've gone through. And that's not fair. I'm never going to be a kumbaya type of boss or friend, but getting some press for the place would thrill them. They're all the way invested, the bad news restaurant is theirs too and it's hard to know how much it grinds on them. I'm not saying that falls to you, I'm honestly not. You just do whatever you're comfortable with for now. I'll give you the big picture today, and if there ends up being a place for it, great. If you can still do one of your foodie stories later, come back out and spend more time with the people who really run this place. Honestly, it's been a good day for old friends to catch up. You should put Topeka in your rotation, get to know this place on your own."

"I'll do that. All of it. I've got a few friends I would bring out here too. Thanks for letting me off the hook, I appreciate it. For real. I wasn't sure how to bring it up but it started hitting me pretty early that I was in over my head. It's a big story and I am not a professional…barely an amateur."

Joe gave me a wink as if to say, 'We're good, kid.' He lit another Vantage and proceeded to give me the true story of how his restaurant got its name. "After my dad passed and Tom and I came to the agreement that we'd keep the place open, but with a completely new direction, coming up with a name quickly became a matter of necessity. There's a whole shit ton of business and banking paperwork that goes into it that you have to deal with, even with the family accountant doing most of it. Tom and

I showed up here one night during the remodeling phase, and the goal was to not leave until we came up with a name. It started off normal; plays on the original Juric's name, something specific to Topeka or Kansas, ethnic history...pretty dry and run of the mill. Eventually it became a battle of wills involving the same goal, but with a case of bourbon that we'd ordered. We could both put it away, probably tried someone's *slivovitz* from their garage still by the time we were ten, so hunkering down and getting shitfaced was no joke. Even that part started slow, we didn't make much progress until we started talking about movies. I basically speak in movie quotes or references all of the time. Tom was exactly the same way. So being brothers, we shared most of the same reference material."

"I'm the same way. I'm always closer to the friends I have who can play that game," I said.

"We started coming up with crazy shit, cracking each other up. In the interest of time I'll give you some highlights, but this shit went on for-*ever*. The first big contender was to call the place Perch. No way you haven't seen *Trading Places*...you remember the part where Aykroyd's girlfriend is going to pick him up in jail or something, and she's on the bench next to some derelict asking about her purse?"

"Oh yeah, slow or drunk guy...Is that your purse?"

"That's a nice purse, exactly!" He chuckled a little. "Well one year Tom and I were out at a family friend's farm pond, this lady who used to make cakes for all of the Croatian weddings, and it was a nice private place to go fish. They had some decent bass in there, but man you had to contend with these little fucking perch, catching and releasing them constantly because they were too small to cook. I happened to catch one that was big, like crappie-sized, so I was putting it on my stringer and Tom looks over at me and dead pans perfectly like a mouth breather 'Is that your perch? That's a nice perch.'...that just fucking destroyed us both, a running joke for *years*."

That was the funniest thing I'd heard in a long time, I was shaking the picnic table laughing.

He kept going. "Another name was Shine. That was a little bit of a darker comedic moment. The original *First Blood*, that was a classic, Rambo was just way fucking cooler in that than any of the sequels. And Brian Dennehy? Forget about it, great movie. We always hated that scene at the end where he starts that whining and crying, you know Troutman wanted to slap him."

I'd seen that movie a million times, the theme song is a classic. "The thing about his friend wants to go home and drive his Chevy? Is that part of the scene? I get my emotional Vietnam movie scenes mixed up."

"That's it!" He gave me the single thumbs up. "The kid comes in the bar going, 'Shine please, shine', and the box is rigged, blows his friend all over him, he tries to hold the guy's guts together and the guy keeps screaming about wanting to go home. We took issue with Rambo falling apart. It was good for the movie storyline to end it that way, but we were big Charles Bronson fans...Rambo was going out like a bitch. The guy keeps screaming about going home and wanting to drive his Chevy, and Rambo is all snot bubbles and says 'With what? I can't find your legs!' all sad and crying. Being movie critics we wanted to keep the same dialogue, but have him go Bronson with it...the guy wants to drive his Chevy and Rambo scolds him, 'With WHAT? Asshole! I can't find your LEGS!' Like hey buddy, you better help me find your fucking legs instead of crying about your goddamn car! That was a running joke forever, veteran dad notwithstanding. The joke would be for one of us to tell the other 'I can't find your fucking LEGS!' if we had lost something, had a stupid question, whatever. But that didn't translate to a restaurant name so we went with Shine."

"I never liked how they felt obligated to throw some ham-handed scene in every movie in an attempt to humanize Rambo," I said, "remember 'Rambo…you…not…expendable…'?"

"Oh hell yes. Just kill. We just want Rambo to kill until he gets to the bad guy who has avoided being killed the entire movie, and then kill the living fuck out of him. Tom and I could never watch a movie together if other people were there, because when we detected weakness in the script it turned into "Mystery Science Theatre" for the rest of the movie. We weren't popular movie watchers with others. Or in general, I guess…almost every word we said was part of an inside joke. We would always find a way to disrupt big family meals with some type of ball busting. We had movies in common and one book…you've read 'To Kill a Mockingbird', right?"

"Oh sure," I told him, "I think I read that right before or after 'Catcher in the Rye' as a kid."

Joe was totally engaged. Going to town on the smokes, and about done with his second beer. "Well one restaurant name that was truly the first runner-up was very literary. We almost went with this one. It sounded good, plus Mockingbird was the one book both of us ever read voluntarily. And we really did read the book. The movie was great, what the fuck was up with that kid who played Dill? But anyway, we were proud of the fact we read a classic without the threat of failing an English class. The Mayella Ewell storyline..."

"That was some heavy shit to write about at that time..." I said.

"For sure. Well, this place was very close to being named The Seven Nickels. You get it?"

I was back to laughing hard. "Yes! Oh my god..."

"It took me a slap year to save seb'm nickels, but I DONE IT!" He did one hell of a Mayella impression. "It wasn't even about her or any deep commentary on the story, we just never knew what in the hell a slap year was. Seriously, what in the fuck is a slap year? It mystifies me to this day. We were drunk as hell, but got all analytical discussing the story, and it always came back to The Seven Nickels. Oh god, if one of us ever thought someone was being condescending it was a race to see who would start in first with 'Your fancy airs don't come to nothin'! Your ma'ammin' and Miss Mayellerin' don't come to nothin'!'

...we wrung all we could out of that book. It was our one book. Should have kept on walking, Tom Robinson. Or at least taken the goddamn thirty-five cents."

"Jesus Joe, that would have been brilliant. I keep a running dialogue in my head all of the time, always movies. The one thing I thought of while you were telling me the names was to call the place Dimi's."

"Where's that from?" He was very curious, someone was joining in his game.

"You remember in the original *The Exorcist*, and the demon is jacking with the priest? It imitates his mom and goes 'Why you do this to me Dimi?' using his childhood nickname."

"OH! Shit yes! That is creepy as shit! Dimi, why you do this? Went back to him dumping her in a home or something? That is actually a good name though, minus the creepy context. Could use it to scare the shit out of Tina. It sounds...ethnic. We actually discussed basing the name on something from that book 'The Jungle', to make it an inside joke but also something kind of Croatian with the meatpacking stereotype. But we'd have to read another book. That was never going to happen."

"Joe, you're from Strawberry Hill and you've never read 'The Jungle'?" I could not comprehend anyone with his family background never reading that particular American classic.

"Nope." He said. "Wasn't as weird as my family not being Catholic."

"So, what made you settle on The Five?" I asked. "The Seven Nickels...that's still killing me."

"It was nothing major at all, just something both of us would always say. I can't even remember the specific comedian who did the bit, back in the Eighties. It may have been Bobcat Goldthwait of all people. It was just this stupid bit about him and his friends growing up, and they were all total dopes. He became the leader because he managed to score a five on some test and blow the rest of them out of the water. Anytime there was a problem or a decision to be made, his friends would look at him and go, 'I don't know man, you're the one who got the five'."

As he told that part of the story, Joe went back into a more serious mood, like he did earlier in the day when he talked about the soup. He leaned farther forward, with his elbows on his thighs, stretching as far as he could as he chose his words.

"The five was our default answer anytime we wanted to push something off on each other. Kind of like calling shotgun. Just look over at the other one and say 'I don't know man, you got the five', or not say anything at all, just hold up your hand to show all five fingers. The ultimate was being fast enough to hold up a five-dollar bill or a nickel before the other one could react. Not sure if you caught it, but I put a five-dollar bill on the wall inside by all of our old books and trophies. I got it from the wallet Tom was carrying when he died, and I stuck it up there before service on the first night we started taking official reservations again. We thought of the name sometime during that night of drinking and we kept coming up with other names, but it was very clear what the place was going to be called. We really had no idea what in the hell we were doing, sitting there in that gutted entryway. Both of our parents were gone. We were really feeling that. No matter how old you get you're still a kid who needs their input or approval, and we'd never have that again. Just two dopes wanting to pass off the responsibility to someone else who wasn't there. It was sad, and stupid, but also exciting...like we got sent back to grade school and had to work our way back."

He flicked his cigarette into the ash can, collected

his bottles and stood up. As he faced away from me to head back into his restaurant, he just said, "Now I'm the one who has The Five."

At 4:15 the dining room was dark but looked ready for service. The tables were set and chairs straightened, some Pandora station quietly played Meatloaf of all things. Joe was at the host station returning a couple of phone calls; one sounded like the bread Moira brought in from the delivery driver earlier was only half of what they asked for. The bar was stacked with a couple of boxes filled with random bottles of liquor that were either going on the shelf or back to the closet. I didn't see any of the servers or Tina at first, but soon I heard people talking in the hallway by the pass and the server station nearest the kitchen. Joe hung up the phone and motioned for me to follow him into the dining room. We sat down at the same table as before, nearest the hallway and kitchen.

"Don't make a mess! They've got it all pretty!" He said, holding his hands up in exaggerated fear. "Family meal going on back there, I'd offer you some but since you're staying for dinner…wait, shit, you haven't eaten since you got up here this morning, have you? If you're starving go back and grab a plate!"

"No, no I'm fine," I told him. "I can wait for dinner. But go ahead if you're not going to get anything between now and the end of service."

"Oh! I'll make time if I want something. Leftover mac and cheese today! It can get a little dry reheating it, but as with most things it's remedied with a fried egg on top. There are worse family meals, trust me."

"I've heard stories about places back home you would not expect to have such terrible family meals, it's hilarious," I said.

"Our food is pretty good to do leftovers, but we switch it up depending on what anyone wants to make or dishes we're working on for a new menu. It's more of a family huddle, you eat back at the station or bar. Never like what you see in movies with all of us at a communal table passing platters of some rustic peasant food, that shit might happen someplace other than movies, I have no idea." He drummed his fingers on the table and switched gears. "Umami! That's one thing I forgot to bring up earlier!"

"That's a good one," I said, "I think your menu is chock full of it."

"I thought of it when I was talking about that first batch of our soup. I was late in the game learning where or even how to keep up on trends. I'd heard of umami but what I read made me think of it in terms of Asian ingredients… soy, kombu, bonito, all of that stuff. It wasn't until someone described it in terms of beef stock that the light went on, oooooohhh NOW I understand…and it has meant a whole lot to me, it's that missing piece. It's the food memory we were talking about that triggered autopilot and kept me from starving when I sat here…exactly right here. At this table."

I looked over his menu, being careful not to disturb the table, and it contained some reliable examples. "Sautéing those mushrooms for the salad, that's a level of flavor you wouldn't normally think of in terms of umami, but it's a biggie."

"The hot sauce a buddy of mine makes has a fermented funk to it that is a personal favorite, I haven't read whatever umami bible is out there but it's valid."

"For sure," I said, "anything with that aged, fermented, earthy background. That's what makes me love charcuterie. Oh, have you ever heard of Red Boat Fish Salt? That is the shit, I think it even mentions umami on the packaging."

"I definitely haven't ever tried that," he said, "I've

used their fish sauce in a few things. Fish sauce is so cheap, and I started buying Red Boat because it was the most expensive. Still really cheap, I don't know, not like I'd know an inferior fish sauce over the Cadillac one."

"They scrape the salt crystals that are left in the barrels after they drain the fish sauce. You have to get some. Trust me. Take a really good dry-aged steak, rub it with some of that salt, put it in your yuppie crockpot and finish on the grill and holy shit you'll see what I mean."

"In!" He gave me that double thumbs up again. "Speaking of steak, one thing that goes as deep as the soup is a dish my mom made growing up. Total Midwestern thing…hamburger steaks with onions, cooked in probably half a bottle of Worcestershire sauce."

"Worcestershire!" I was excited he brought that up. "That's our soy sauce! That triggers so much good food memory. That and liquid smoke whenever there was a brisket roasting in the oven."

"Oh yeah…walking in the house and hitting a wall of that smell. Hamburger grease, onion and Worcestershire would hang in the air for days. My mom would cook the hell out of those onions too, totally black at the edges, sliding in fat on your plate, hard to even get one on your fork."

"That stuff is my secret ingredient when my wife plans turkey burgers for dinner. Inside, outside, all over. Jerry these are great! Uh-huh…it makes anything great."

"Turkey burgers!" He sat back in his chair and laughed. "You've come a long way! If I'm understanding umami correctly, you'll know you've reached enlightenment when you're riddled with fucking gout."

We chatted for a little while longer about family classics and Midwestern cuisine. We decided any trends that mattered were from opportunists who found a way to rebrand something everyone grew up with in one form or another. Umami was just a way to monetize emotional blackmail. There was some laughter and activity back at the pass, but we were still the only ones in the dining room. I was starting to pick up cues from Joe's body language whenever he was about to shift gears and get serious. He took a big breath and exhaled through his nose, slid down a little in his chair and took a moment to silently focus on a spot on the table. He wiped at something on the tablecloth that I could not see.

"Between this table and the banquette, that's where I spent most of my time right after Tom died. I don't know if it was a weird subliminal thing that pushed me here or totally by chance, but out of all of our customers and all of the stories I've discussed, this is where our one true regular always sits. My dad's friends are in here constantly, but they don't count. I'm talking about someone who has eaten here since my parents ran the place, and has been faithful to this day. Watching him has taught me about perspective. About what a good day means. You know what a good day means?"

I assumed he was being rhetorical, so I made enough eye contact to acknowledge he should keep talking.

"Mr. Novak and his wife came here *all* the time. Sat right here whenever the table was open. Friends with my parents from way back, for all I know they were the first people me or Tom ever served a plate of food when we were young. They were old to us back then. Know what I mean? Old people who have just always been old?"

"Oh, for sure," I nodded my head, "once in a while I'll be shocked to find out an old person from the church where I grew up is actually still alive. Seeing them at a funeral that isn't theirs. It's weird."

"That was Mr. and Mrs. Novak for us. Between

always seeing them here and them being older, I never even thought of the two of them as real people with real problems…they were a TV show or something to me even into my thirties. They were reliable, and always friendly. Always having a good day. Our parents must have doled out all of the intel to them, because me and Tom would get a birthday card or a congrats card for something once in a while when they came in. The sweetest people when my folks died, when my dad passed they made sure to let us know they understood and supported us no matter what we decided to do with the place. When they came in for their first dinner at The Five, that's when they were finally real to me…that meant a lot."

He walked over to the bar to get a beer and a Coke. When he handed me the soda can he gestured at the table with his free hand and pointed at the can, reminding me I didn't want to get anything on the tablecloth. There had to be a good dining room etiquette story involving his staff, but that would have to wait for another day. He kept talking about his favorite regulars.

"They were pumped that now they could make a reservation and book their same table. Out of habit I guess, it's the worst table in the house. I got a single brass 'Reserved' sign just for them, it was like I'd gotten them their own red carpet...they loved it. And on that went, they'd be in once a week without fail. When Tom died, the same thing, they were in my corner no matter what. So obviously they were some of the first people we had back in here before I had even decided we'd stay open. And then Mrs. Novak got sick...cancer, just like my mom. I didn't even know about it for a long time, they were still in here and just as sweet as always. I noticed Mr. Novak would always mention whether or not his wife was having a good day if it was just me and him talking, like I was in the know. I didn't want to ask but it became obvious soon enough. I'd watched that process. It's fucking heartless. The victories you grasp onto that define a good day get smaller and smaller but it's all you've got. This restaurant was a constant that they had for so many years, and they weren't going to miss coming here. She didn't miss but two weeks I think. Date night, right here. I just had him call and tell me what he thought she could eat or was even in the mood for because of treatments and medication, and I'd have it ready. And in the middle of dying she was so grateful, we made a big deal about her getting stuff that wasn't even on the menu and she loved it."

Joe shifted in his chair, moved the silverware nearest him back and forth like he was finding the right spot for it. I tried not to put too much thought into it, no spiritual symbolism or anything, but I suddenly realized for the first time that from where Joe was sitting, his back to the kitchen entrance, the pictures of his family behind him flanked him on both sides. His dad and mom on his right, brother on his left. Once I saw it I couldn't stop seeing it; the three of them over his shoulders. I'm not a superstitious person, but it stayed with me for the rest of the time we sat there.

"You never think in terms of the moment in your life when cutting your own food or feeding yourself becomes the high point of your good day. And not only your pain, but the pain of the person feeding you, after all those years with you watching you falter and shrink. Losing you piece by piece. All of your time so consumed with it that you don't even have time to process it. I guess that's good though. I know staying busy is what keeps you sane. I watched those people and kept this hope that it would all turn around, and it would be back to like it was with the birthday cards and making a production of that fucking Reserved sign. I didn't want to get used to losing people. Inside you're cheering and you're dreading. And then it's the day when Mr. Novak comes in all alone. Because this place still makes sense. This table. He never misses a week."

Listening to Joe made me think about how I'd spent the better part of my life narrowing down people and places that mattered, doing my best to have "my guy" for any situation. Restaurants, home repairs, car dealers, dentists...everything vetted by word of mouth from people I already knew. Date nights and special occasions exist within a very, very small sphere of options. I only spend that time someplace where the people who operate it would be welcome at my table...so everything Joe said about his friends made sense. So many places want to be known for feeling like home, but that's just advertising. It's only home if trust goes both ways, and the cost of trust is shared. There has to be an investment made by all parties that leaves some figurative blood on the table.

"I think it's instinct to seek some kind of routine during times of grief." I told him.

"For sure, for sure...people want to romanticize it, all that better to have loved and lost shit. When your guts are torn out and your world has ended, that's the kind of shit people say to blow you off so that they don't have to deal with you. People who ask how you're doing but don't want an honest answer," he said.

"Or make it all about them. That's the finishing move of a whole segment of people in the Bible Belt. The testimony. They get to talk about themselves. Or make a production out of being a great listener. You know this Joe, you're here in revival land!" I raised my hands like we were in church.

Joe rolled his eyes and smiled. "I've always been a target, I guess being Croatian but not Catholic makes you fair game for Bible thumpers. If you're Catholic there isn't any hope for you so they leave you alone. With the notoriety of the restaurant, sometimes you get 'All these folks need is Jesus!' from people. And that's cool, I have no problem with most church people. I'm not an atheist, but I don't want to act like a phony. I don't want to be oblivious to how transparent my motives are every time I talk to someone. It's not genuine. Inquiring about whether or not my brother was right with the Lord when he died? And counting shit like that as ministry? Not saying two words to me on any day someone *hasn't* just died in my family? And then suddenly not leaving me the fuck alone? Lazy, entitled assholes."

"Grief is selfish, Joe. You have to let your light shine," I joked.

"Ha! God won't give you more than you can handle. That's pretty twisted when you think about how big of a sadist that must make God. Instead of just wrecking you, he'll keep you right at the edge without finishing the job, you don't quite go insane or die. People sell it like that is where true love is found. I understand what people are trying to say, but they sound like they repeat it so much they've never taken the time to understand what a complete fucking asshole they sound like. Then bonus points for them when you call them a fucking asshole...because martyr complex. You've proven them right. They go back and share the testimony with their hive." He raised his hand and cocked his head in the universal 'I dunno' gesture.

"Yeah Joe, people flock to whatever belief gives them the fastest, simplest answers to life's biggest questions. They just happened to be born into the exact right version of the correct religion every single time. They're junkies who get so high on thinking they're winning souls that nothing else about you matters to them. That might require actual work."

"I'm not saying people need to let themselves go nuts and not reach out for help, the whole Catholic nobility of suffering is a load of shit," he continued, "but eventually you either live through grief or you make it something it's not and become someone you're not supposed to be."

Joe grabbed his phone and started thumbing through websites, after about a minute, he put the phone down and looked over at me and said, "I usually just get pissed off thinking about all of this religious denial of grief shit, but last year I ran across this picture in my news feed that changed the way I think about all of it. I've lost every person in my immediate family within the past ten years, so when I say this made an impact, you have to understand what I mean. It broke me in half. I was going to show you, but you'll just have to remember to look it up when you get home. Or not. It's the single strongest image I've ever seen. Ever. The kind of thing you can't ever forget. But that's good. At least it was for me."

"I'll absolutely look it up. What is it?" I asked, a little fearful. Neither of us was the type of man to preface anything like that lightly.

"This family in England, the dad was a photographer maybe," he began, leaning forward with his forearms crossed on the table, "they had a four-year-old girl who had been diagnosed with cancer. Neuroblastoma,

I think. I've never been married, and have no kids, but that alone is hard for me to think about."

"Yeah, that is real horror," I told him, "there's nothing I love more than my wife and daughter, and thinking of something like that is like trying to comprehend what is past the known universe. Your mind can't grasp it."

"Well, as it got close to the end, her dad took a picture and put it online. It's the one I just happened to see and for whatever reason I go back to it from time to time…I don't even know why, it tears me apart the same way every time. I mean, you see that stuff, social media is full of sick kids, sad pet stories…but usually it's framed in some bittersweet way that's meant to be life-affirming or something. But he didn't do that. He took a picture of the pain."

"Jesus…," was all I could add, not sure if it was something I could even bring myself to look at.

"Yeah…in black and white, this skinny little girl with long hair, an oxygen tube in her nose, tears coming out of her eyes, eyes and lips clenched as tightly as she could get them, body completely stiff, rigid with pain, dark veins on her torso, frozen there in that picture. Her whole world was that pain, more pain than the rest of us would feel in our entire lifetimes. Her short life and that's all she knew."

He sat back in his chair, hands in his lap. "You think of her family frantically trying to fit in all of the love they would ever be able to give her, the only love she'd ever know. Ever. She was never going to fall in love, walk to the bus stop for school, make new friends, hit the snooze button five times before finally getting up for work. Never know or understand anything beyond the hurting, no concept of peace until everything finally ended. Four years old. I sit and wonder what ever made her happy, if she ever just got to be a little girl before she got sick. It doesn't make me grateful for what I've got, there isn't some big life lesson in it other than life makes no fucking sense. There's no solution there, no canned scripture or mantra you leave with her parents. Like you said, it's too big to comprehend. I like what we do here. I am grateful for what I have and what people can get from it. But there is a depth to life you can only hope you never have to learn for yourself."

"There aren't any words for that," I said, worn out from what he described, "anyone who tries to draw a comparison isn't worth listening to…the sheer amount of horror stories that get thrown at us every day just turn into data, white noise…"

"He stopped all of that noise with that picture…maybe that's why I go back to it. It's too big to figure out, so in its own dark way it keeps me grounded. I feel like not having answers is okay."

Tina stuck her head around the corner for a second, and one of the servers walked into the other end of the dining room from the bar. Joe stood up and checked to make sure the table was in order.

"Well," he said, "as uplifting and light-hearted as this has been, they're going to toss us out for lineup. Tina and I usually go over the reservations, cover administrative stuff. She can do it today, I'm going to run down and suit up real quick."

It was a little over forty minutes until the doors opened, and I was sitting at the bar while Joe went downstairs to change clothes. I was mentally exhausted from bouncing back and forth between the bonding that comes from all of the laughing and the kind that comes from processing all of the emotion…mine, Joe's, and what I was able to pick up about his staff. I had no emotional investment when I left my home that morning. Then, in my attempt to take in everything he was telling me and fretting about getting a story, I didn't realize how full my brain was until I came to a dead stop after listening to Joe's stories about the Novaks and that little girl. I had my own stories, my share of loss in my life, but my emotional overload coupled with no food all day gave me an appreciation for exactly what it was that brought people to The Five. It reinforced my respect for Joe and his staff for keeping at it without recognition beyond a small town. It made me appreciate my friends back home. I don't put much value on knowing a lot of people for the sake of having someone to talk to, so it's rare to find a group as genuinely cool as the industry friends I've made. Everyone is a little fucked up. They have a certain patina to their character that can only exist under the right pressure. It's enlightening when you begin to see past the characters they have to play for the sake of hospitality. You have to get close enough to learn first-hand the impacts of most not having health insurance, or how much work has to get done before and after your two hours at your table. The general ass-busting to mop the bar and dining room after First Friday clusterfuck or getting a lung full of degreaser cleaning the hoods. You learn quickly that the chefs who run the top kitchens in the most expensive restaurants usually aren't close to being wealthy, and other than samples during line up your server may or may not ever get to sit down and have the same meal they just brought you. When you see an owner's cute baby in the dining room with them and their spouse, it's probably because there is work they both have to get done and also this might be the most time they all spend with each other all week. As I sat at the bar, all of those things reminded me I had it pretty good. My trip to Topeka expanded my world a little more. The Five had become part of what made me care about that unpredictable and constantly evolving community.

Tina and Cesar were with the servers in the dining room, reading over some reservation details and staff schedules for the next week. Someone brought up being out of town for Valentine's Day, which made me wonder what that shift was like at The Five. It's a shit show everyplace else, right up there with New Year's Eve. Total amateur night. Regulars stay home while their favorite spots churn out well-done steaks and some version of lobster. They turn tables as quickly as possible, hoping things don't get backed up if the most unoriginal men in town propose to their girlfriends en masse. I had no idea how it went down at The Five. My best guess was that it became just another restaurant with spillover guests after every place in town booked solid.

Moira went back and forth to the bathroom a couple of times to retrieve bottles from the liquor closet. Then she took a trip downstairs with the ice bucket, bringing it back up and setting it on the edge of the well without dumping it in. She polished a lowball glass and kept her eyes on it while she started to speak. It took me a couple of moments to realize she was talking to me. After what Joe told me about her and witnessing their interactions, it was a bit of a shock but also a welcome surprise. It made me feel closer to the place, it helped to justify such a quick emotional investment.

"So you grew up with Joe?" she asked.

"Yeah, yeah for a while, till he moved out here. We're from the same neighborhood."

"He has been happy you were coming here. This is good to see him sit down. It's good to see him be funny," she told me.

"He's a funny guy. This place is something else, the history here. Sorry I haven't been out sooner."

She put the glass down, and looking at me asked, "You're writing a story?"

"I don't know," I told her, "I was planning on it, but this place is about a lot of things. Too many for what I originally hoped to write. I don't know what I was expecting."

"Whatever it is, make it good." She was serious. "He hasn't invited anyone else. Just you. Every other writer he said 'no.'"

"What other writers?" I was confused. "He told me I was the first person to ask him after the newspaper article."

"Oh, he told you that?" She shook her head slightly, picked up a different glass and began polishing it.

"Him, his brother, his dad…all the same. Hard workers and afraid of losing control if they let people help them. Joe needs something that isn't this place. I tell him that. It's not good for him, every day here and then alone in his home. Ask him about his girlfriend. Someone who isn't dead. You do that."

She filled the glass she'd been polishing with ice, placed a napkin in front of me and set the glass on it. Then she walked to the other end of the bar to retrieve a can of Coke. She opened it on her way back over to me, and made eye contact as she poured. She gave me a little nod, and I wasn't sure what that meant. It could have been intimidation, here's to your health, or a simple acknowledgement that we had an agreement. Whatever it was, nothing about Moira offered the slightest sense that she was fucking around.

A couple of minutes later, Joe walked back into the bar, buttoning up the last couple of buttons on his chef jacket. "Ta-DA!" he said, with a flourish of his hands.

"Very nice!" I told him. "Not bad for an old guy from back home. Much nicer than prison blues."

"I know! We don't have a Whole Foods for me to walk through wearing this, or I'd be set!" He laughed and smoothed the front of it.

"So Joe, I forgot to ask if you had a girlfriend." It just came out of my mouth.

He looked at me, then at Moira. She quickly busied herself polishing another glass. He looked back at me, and then shifting his gaze right back at Moira he said slowly and deliberately, "Why no, Jerry. I don't have a girlfriend."

Joe walked over to the bar and sat down directly in front of her, she had still not looked up. I took the stool next to him, wondering what I'd just started.

"I never know what music to play in here," he said, "can't be too loud, but classical is out. Moira keeps a nice balance."

She looked up at him for one second, then went back to straightening the bar top.

"If you weren't here, she'd be jamming out all day to one thing or another. Totally forgets people might suddenly walk in on her. Not a care in the world. Moira, you still a big fan of Alanis Morrissette?" he asked her.

Her eyes locked on him, "You don't."

Joe put his hands up and with mock bewilderment said, "What? You're a music fan. You can't keep your feet still! You love it!"

She looked at him for a few seconds, then went to the other end of the bar. I wasn't going to ask about it that day, but I would absolutely get the skinny on Moira's apparent solo dancefest Joe had discovered.

"Jerry! I thought of something when I was downstairs. Coincidentally, it has to do with women. I actually learned this from a cook a few years back, but every cook since then has confirmed some variation in the kitchens where they've worked. The configuration here is tough, open kitchens work way better so you need an assist from a server sometimes, but an important part of kitchen morale is the ability to alert cooks if a very hot chick is in the building."

"You have a system?" I asked.

"Oh yeah. You have to know already how we keep an eye on our guests. You fucking know how it is. Most of it is purely administrative, but if you're lingering too long on a busy night or keep sending shit back, your ears burn for a reason. Nobody is fucking with your food or anything like that, but you're under a microscope. That's just how it is."

I laughed, "Yeah. You don't dine in a vacuum. I just try to be the guy dishing the compliments. Service people have some fucked up humor."

"Yup," he said, "and we talk about the same shit every person talks about. Kitchens are especially rough. And I've had female cooks, fantastic ones, and fair is fair...if some ripped guy who looks like he jammed a tree trunk down his pants walks in, we can't have a discriminatory hot guest alert system."

"It's only right Joe!" I said, "Topeka is really catching up with the rest of the world!"

"Damn straight. So basically, how the hot babe alert works is by table number, seat number here at the bar...the bar is the number one series, one through six. The bar tables at the banquette are the ten series, then the three rows of tables in the dining room are twenty, thirty and forty. You can account for the seat numbers, but normally it doesn't have to be that specific. Whoever the spotter is relays her exact location back here. We use rice; the number of minutes until the rice is done tells you what table to check out when you get a chance. We don't have rice. I can't remember us ever cooking rice for any menu, and we probably never will now...it's a solid system, a tradition."

"Ah, okay," it was making sense to me, "so second table back at the far wall would be forty-two minutes."

"Correct! If I see one of them leave and come back grinning, or a server comes in to whisper to one of them I can just ask 'How we coming on that rice?', and someone will answer 'Forty-two minutes, Chef!' Or they can just volunteer the info by announcing the time left on the rice. There isn't a lot of bullshit talk back there during service, I'm a heads-down boss, but tradition is important."

"Joe, that reminds me of 'What's happening with those sausages, Charlie? Five minutes, Turkish.'"

He laughed, "It was two minutes five minutes ago! Yeah, me and Cesar are the only two cooks I know who haven't run that one into the ground."

Hunger was really starting to kick in. I got a big whiff of smoky onion and then bacon coming from the kitchen. The meeting in the dining room was wrapping up and Joe grabbed some Windex from the bottom of the server station and took it into the bathroom. When he returned a minute later, he walked over and shook the ice bucket that Moira left on the edge of the well, but he didn't dump it in. After walking over and glancing at the reservation notebook, he came back and sat at the bar.

"So, you and Moira obviously talked, and that's cool, when it comes to her you just got the highest form of praise." Joe said, "She wants me to get married. Thinks it will keep me from being such a morose bastard. Isn't that right, dear?"

"You will do what you're going to do." Moira responded, still at the other end of the bar.

"Jerry, you're married, what's your take?"

That was a big question. "Well, in a nutshell it's great. You have a partner who loves you. You have each other's back. It's work, though. You just do your best, when in doubt talk about whatever it is that's bothering either of you. Having a kid is the other side of the moon, though. It's the most fantastic thing in the world to have them in your life, and it's also the most terrifying. It's both of those things, all the time. All the time. You just try not to fuck them up."

"I doubt I'd still have kids," he said, "too old

now, tied down every evening. And I'm not one of those professional bachelors, I don't have anything against marriage. Watched my brother go through the most hellish divorce. Crazy ex who already had two crazy kids. Holy shit, that put me off the idea for a while. I'm not celibate, fuck that. I just can't do the whole auditioning process. And my track record is pretty fucking bad...I'm the one constant in this shit-pile of family tragedy."

"You think it's some kind of Juric curse?" I asked.

"I don't know what in the hell it is, but it would make that speed dating shit awkward as fuck. My family history? Oooh not great. May as well just be like 'My family isn't the ONLY thing about me that's dead, ladies!' and point at my crotch, all smiles. Maybe don't print that. The dead dick thing. I'm not quite there yet. I've got a few years."

I laughed at that. "Sorry Joe, it's all or nothing. The dead dick thing goes in the story."

He shook his head and gave me a look like Moe before he slaps Curly. "In my twenties I took it all too seriously, like every girl I dated had to be the one. You mistake having the most obvious shit in common with compatibility. I beat my head into the wall there for years.

Sad ass heartbreak…you drink your way through it and listen to your secret stash of breakup songs. After a while it gets beaten out of you, and you either live and learn or pretend women are all terrible. But you spend so much of your time as the dumbass thinking- huge boobs and she's seen a Jarmusch movie! This is the real thing!"

"I know what you mean, I'm glad I didn't get married until I was older," I shared with him, "it's easier to find real values in common instead of just hobbies. I'd have five or six divorces under my belt otherwise."

Joe looked back over at Moira and said, "But this one over here! Mrs. Subtle! A girl who worked here for a while is who she's talking about. We're still friends. Never my girlfriend. Not because I'm the honorable boss who would never pull that shit, I just never have any idea where I stand with women. And she's got the potential to turn me into a dumbass."

Still at the end of the bar, Moira snorted and said, "Short trip for you…"

Joe looked over, rocked his head and shoulders back and forth very slightly, and responded with Alanis lyrics, "Moira! I want you to know…that I'm hap-pee for you…"

"No. I said you don't do that." She shot him a quick glare and then stared towards the front door.

I did not have the time or inclination to feed whatever the situation was between Joe and his work mom. I went back to what he had been talking about. "Joe, I'm the exact same way. I was always the fat kid, and between that and the fear of hell from church I completely missed however flirting works."

"Oh, I'm clueless!" he said. "She'll mention what made some guy she went out with a horrible kisser and I'll over-analyze the shit out of it, but never react or follow the thread. We talk all the time and I am still not sure whether or not she's just being nice to me because she thinks I'm slow."

For some reason that struck me as funnier than it was and set me off laughing.

"No, I'm serious!" Joe insisted. "I had a new girlfriend once who was spending the night for the first time, and when I came out of the bathroom and found her in my bed I said something like 'So...is it cool I'm sleeping in here too?'"

That did not stop my laughter, but I did my best

to pull it together and asked, "So what sent you down the path this time? Just curious, it's obviously a whole thing with you."

He stretched against the stool back and crossed his arms. "When someone starts working here, just to get a read on their personality I'll ask the Beatles versus Stones question."

"Stones," I said.

"Precisely," he looked at me and nodded, "I appreciate the genius of The Beatles, but I don't connect with them. It's not in my DNA."

"Same here," I told him, "Bands like The Beatles, or someone like Springsteen, I honestly admire them and respect how people dedicate themselves to their music. I just don't relate. Probably all the rock and metal we grew up on."

"Maybe, but I'm also kind of like that with Led Zeppelin...and Springsteen's singing sounds like he needs to take the most urgent shit but can't push it out. *Anyway*, I asked her the big question when she started here and she thought for a second and answered, 'The Cars.'"

"Oh, ok. I get it now," I told him.

"You get it? Right? Like you watch *Chasing Amy* now and you can see what a horribly shitty movie it is, but when you first saw it and Ben Affleck gives the whole I love you speech, as a younger guy you don't see how sad and creepy it is. You thought it was powerful and romantic. So now as an older, somewhat wiser man when a girl switches up a major question with The Cars, it hits something inside you that warns you not to pull a Chasing Amy. Thank god she didn't say Cheap Trick. I'd either be married or still drunk."

"I'm no scientist, but she's also hot, right?" I asked.

"Man, it isn't about that...you dick." He looked at me with contempt, but also grinned and relented. "When she gets off her shift these days, and climbs down from her perch high above Notre Dame, her one good eye is so pretty...yes, asshole, she's hot. She's very attractive and would hold her own talking about any of this. She makes me stupid. She's younger than me but not creepy younger. We have good talks."

"So what is the problem?"

"Yes, what is the problem?" Moira jumped back in for more. It was obviously a big sticking point with her.

Joe looked over and started singing, "It's like raaaaiiinnn on your wedding day!"

She threw down her bar towel and stormed off toward the kitchen. Joe's serenade followed her out, "It's a free riiiiiide but you already paid!"

He stopped singing as soon as she was out of sight, but he waited a moment like he expected her to run back in with a retort. He said, "It's not a problem really, but when too much clicks it's hard to trust it...it's a big risk, and with all my baggage and running this place it's scary to bump into someone who likes you but in no way *needs* you. Someone without an agenda who makes you feel happy just to be around them, and you always want to know more about them. We were here late one night after service, I'd known her for a week maybe, and after a couple of drinks I said let's cut all the bullshit and get right down to talking about the worst days of our lives. So we did. And we are definitely broken in a lot of the same places. But is that good or is it bad?"

"It's good that you can talk about it," I said, "but I get what you mean. I know a lot of people in recovery, and when two of them start dating it's a little like what you're saying. Does the bad stuff make you stronger together or are you setting yourselves up? For me personally, I'd go live in a cave before I dated another drunk."

Joe got up and walked around to stand on the other side of the bar across from me. He grabbed another beer out of the cooler and opened it.

"And then there's the pressure from people," he cocked his head back at the kitchen, "they tell you how it's so cute, it has to be a love connection. My mom must have given Moira her marching orders to find me a wife. And my people mean well, they do. And I appreciate it, but my paranoid nature wonders if they're really seeing what they think, or if they're just seeing two people entertaining each other with their deeply developed defense mechanisms. Peeking over our giant emotional walls just enough to communicate. I'm most comfortable in a friends with benefits situation, maybe that sounds sad and lonely, I'm just being honest. But she's an outlier. It would have to be all or nothing with her, and we're a lot of the same kinds of crazy. The knives come out eventually, and as goofy and young as the good stuff makes me feel…when it got bad it would be very fucking bad."

"Goddamn dude," I said, "you really are one

morose old bastard. You read any Bukowski?"

"Nope," he answered, "I've heard of him, saw *Barfly*, but unless he has something in 'To Kill a Mockingbird' I haven't read his stuff."

"He did a poem called 'Quiet Clean Girls in Gingham Dresses,' I think that's the name. If you ever venture outside Harper Lee, look that up."

Joe walked over to the closet by the server station and retrieved a package of folded paper towels; the type that fit into a bathroom dispenser. He came back and put them next to the ice bucket that still sat there, and took a pull from his beer.

"I think our generation got set up," he looked over towards the dining room but didn't seem to focus on anything, "we had the best teen romantic comedies but guys couldn't like that shit in public. Know what I mean? John Hughes totally fucked us."

"Yes!" I laughed and added, "I saw *Some Kind of Wonderful* at State Drive-In when it came out, and that was the best thing I'd ever seen in my life. I loved Mary Stuart Masterson with all my heart! And Jenny Wright in *The Chocolate War*...oh my god. But I know what you mean. If you so much as admitted you listened to a hair band like Cinderella instead of real metal, you risked getting left behind or ditched while perpetrating some kind of caper. I was super drunk once and merely mentioned a song by that band The Outfield, and never lived that down...Grade A little bitch."

"The Eighties perfected the movie montage." Joe smiled and then began to laugh. "When I'm driving down the road thinking about this girl, my brain spits out these sarcastic music montages...dysfunctional dopes finding love or something. I thought of one the other day when I was going over stuff to tell you, and that dude in *Trading Places* kept coming to mind."

"Purse guy?" I asked.

"Yes! It was bizarre, both of us were dimwitted as hell, sitting next to each other on that jail bench. She smells something horrible, looks over at me and in that 'nice purse' voice asks 'Did you just shit your pants?', and I turn to her slowly and, same voice, reply 'I thought...we could shit them together'. Then slow-mo montage starts! Guitar builds and you get a lump in your throat because it's Boston! The intro to 'More Than a Feeling!' Lovefest through the whole song, shit-pants couple laughing and exploring the city. And everyone we run into is just cheering us on. It ends with us on a beach, for an unexplained reason because the rest takes place *here*, but the sun is going down as the song ends and we've got our hands clasped spinning round and round with our heads back laughing like idiots. Then you can tell we're one second away from puking from all the spinning, and it cuts to the next scene."

"*That*...is fucking weird, man." I admired, and kind of feared, the level of detail. "Boston is a nice touch! Another good one would be if you looped the guitar intro to 'Sweet Child O' Mine' and used only that until the very end and closed out with Axl doing the last 'sweet child o' miiiiine...'"

"Excellent!" He laughed and finished the last of his beer and tossed the bottle in the recycle bin. "I make up crazy shit to avoid making a move one way or the other. The sick part of me keeps waiting for the moment when I stop liking her just being herself. It's stupid, juvenile. Waiting for some imaginary betrayal of trust where you expected her to love the same song you're embarrassed to love, but she hated it. Something that ridiculous. I'm not being literal, I'm not recording a fucking make or break mix tape for her. I'm not going to be outside her window hissing 'Love me! LOOOVE MEEEE!' Risk isn't something that scares me in every other part of my life, but this terrifies me. But we all deserve it, right? The cheesy John Hughes moments come from somewhere don't they?"

"I don't know, Joe." I shook my head and shrugged. "But Moira seems pretty damn invested in this situation."

"You think? She means well. She's family. But I have to fuck with her. Maybe if me and the girl get matching tattoos that will be enough of a lifetime bond for everyone to leave me alone."

"If not there's always reincarnation, Joe. Maybe the two of you will get lucky and meet again when you're young and stupid."

"It may have to come to that, or trust that we're shacked up in a parallel universe." he said, "She's moving to Milwaukee for another cooking gig in a few months."

I thought about it for a few seconds and told him, "Well, that gives you a little time to compile all the movies where the guy tries to catch the girl at the airport before she leaves him forever. It's no *Trading Places* mouth breather shitgasm or anything, but you'll get some good angst out of it."

"You're a dick, Jerry. I respect it. Not enough to write you into any of my montages, but you'll be the first person I call when I get shot at the airport for trying to stop a flight to Milwaukee."

-9-

It was almost time for the doors to open and the servers were doing last minute straightening of the tables, dimming the dining room and lighting candles. Joe was at the host station with Tina, looking at the reservations and listening to her recap of lineup. It had been a long day, but I felt like I got quite a bit more than I expected. The Five was first and foremost a family restaurant; much different in scope and execution than what Joe's parents created, but without question still a family place. Everything he shared with me was carefully placed within a context that made the truth sound less fantastic than the urban myth that had been building since his reopening. I understood why he did it, but his lack of confidence in his ability as a chef was tremendously offset by the amount of thought and labor he put into his family's remaining legacy. I liked Joe. I liked the way he told his story, and felt grateful for the opportunity to hear it. I wanted to dig into his crazy menu and keep coming back whenever I could to spend time watching everything play out. The truth was much simpler and infinitely more meaningful than the legend.

I waited at the bar while he hurried to get last

minute tasks accomplished. He finished looking over the
reservations and came over behind the bar to finally dump
that bucket of melting ice into the well. Then he grabbed
the bundle of paper towels he retrieved earlier and took
them into the bathroom. While he was in there, Cesar
appeared near the kitchen door, rolling a speed rack
against the wall. Joe came out about a minute later with a
small trash bag. He put it on the floor at the end of the bar
and walked into the kitchen just long enough to roll the
same speed rack out of sight. Once he was back in the bar
he picked up a clean towel and quickly wiped the surface
of the bar starting at the end nearest the front door. He
didn't say anything to anyone the whole time, he was
focused and moved quickly. After the bar top he plucked
the bag of bar trash from the can, threw the smaller bag
from the bathroom inside of it, and carried it over to the
closet where he retrieved a broom. "Rituals!" he said,
looking at me and nodding his head toward the front door.
With his hands full I rushed over to open it for him and
we stepped outside. "Be right back!" he told me, handing
me the broom and taking the bag of trash around the
building to the dumpster. When he returned, he took the
broom and held it in front of himself with two hands,
bristles pressed down against the concrete as he leaned in
slightly and rocked a bit. It had gotten dark. My earlier

suspicions were confirmed; the bulb over the front steps and the three tall lights in the parking lot were the only things lit up on that street with the exception of an occasional passing car. It was chillier with the sun down but still unseasonably warm. We stood quietly for about a minute.

"I'm glad you came out today," he told me, "I hope you got what you came for...got some answers about the place."

"Grateful for the opportunity, Joe. Legend aside, you've got a solid business. You've got direction, employees you can trust, and people like eating your food."

"In some ways the place is like therapy, or busy work so you don't realize you need therapy." He said. "It's good to make people happy though. I don't want to get oohs and aahs. I feel lucky that people trust me with their meals, I just want to make them comfortable. When you're in pain, minutes kill you. Nothing we've got will solve that, but if we can pass some time, take some of those minutes so you can live a little easier, that's the highest level of my profession. At least in my mind. I don't know. Maybe I put too much weight on how everything came together."

"Look," I told him, "I don't see this place as divinely inspired, I also don't think you have to over-analyze it. Maybe it's fate, maybe it's luck, maybe it's simply the fact that salt, fat, warmth, wine and a comfy seat are just fucking magical. Period."

"True, true." He nodded his head, still propped up against his broom. "I like being able to say, this is what food is. This is what cooking is. That connection. Not all the cheap clichés about soulfulness and fucking death row meals. Seriously, how many of those idiots have even seen the inside of a jail? Every single fucking meal is your death row meal. Think about that. Spoiled assholes. I'll take genuine sorrow over their manufactured joy. No question."

That last comment got Joe fired back up. He started sweeping the spot right in front of him, going back and forth between checking his work and looking at me as he spoke. There was absolutely no dirt or leaves on the front steps, I assumed it had to be some kind of tradition even before he told me.

"You do things that force you to remember people." He kept sweeping, thinking between sentences.

"You can't let it all become nothing. You lose people but you have rituals that make you remember. This right here. Every day. All that shit inside, I don't even have to tell my people. They know it's coming. I look over our reservations even though I don't really need to. The bucket of ice sits there for a couple of hours before I dump it. That's what happened, Moira just let that shit sit one day. So I dump that, I go put paper towels in the bathroom, Windex the mirror, and grab the trash. I am very compulsive when it comes to the kitchen being prepped…especially with the speed racks. I need to walk in there and see even numbers, four, four, four, four, all the way down, clean sheet pans on the racks. I wipe down the bar, make sure there isn't anything sitting on it, get the bar and bathroom trash gathered and grab this broom." He held it up, like a trophy. "I sat and forced myself to remember all of this stuff. Every action, every minute. I do them every day. All of the things I did right before I watched my brother leave the last time I ever saw him. Normal day, he was heading out for a while and I was holding down the fort. I stood here sweeping right before service. Watched him walk to his car, off into the dark. Didn't think anything else about it."

Joe backed up and started sweeping the area right

around the front door, just past the heavy winter curtains. "Surviving all of those horrible minutes! Does this routine make me feel better or make me feel worse? I don't even know. I just do it and hopefully someone will pull up, walk in the door sooner than later because that's when I go back inside and we start it all up. This routine stays the same, but the way it ends and service starts is always new. You keep the routine until something changes, and hope the change isn't something that makes you rethink everything. When I lost my brother the first thing I learned was that everything you do from that point forward is the first time you've ever done it. Your life is completely new, everything has been cut apart and has to grow back. The first shower when you feel the water for the first time, first phone call, first time you drive your car, have a meal, smoke a cigarette, watch a movie…all of the reference points have changed. You aren't the same person. It goes on until you've done almost everything in your life again for the first time. That's when things seem normal. Until you do something you never even thought of. Either something you forgot and you do it again for the first time, or something you've never done…and you miss them in a completely different way. You'll never be able to share it with them, so you live it for them. Jerry, you remember waiting for your parents to come home when you were old enough to stay alone for the first time?"

"Yeah," I had to think about it, and nodded my head, "it was probably summer, the first time I didn't get a babysitter…trusted to be on my own."

Joe stopped sweeping the steps. He put the broom against the wall and his hands in his pockets, leaned forward a bit and either smiled or winced. "Well, you'd hear a thousand cars pass your house every day, but somehow you know which one belongs to your parents. The tires or the engine, something about it sets it apart. Things like that are programmed in you, some things since your earliest childhood…little sounds, movements, gestures, facial tics that you share with someone, catching an expression in the mirror that belonged to someone else first…a million little connections cut out of you in one massive wound. Cut out so fast there's no way you can take a mental inventory, or even know how you would do such a thing…how you'd even try. But you notice things that are missing. You may not even know exactly what it is, but you feel something familiar isn't there anymore. Those things become fewer and fewer as time goes on. You get back to normal, but it's a new kind of normal that eventually becomes more than sadness."

He looked at me, cocked his head and raised his eyebrows in a way that told me to think about what he was saying, then he continued. "That's how grief does its thing. You can put it off or try to deny it, it doesn't matter though…everybody is different but they lose everything the same way. Some people even deserve it. Some don't. If you're lucky you're just stuck where I was…thinking about the last time you said I love you. And the last time you didn't. But the game is over. Things fade. It hasn't been long enough yet but I know that Tom's voice will fade, his face will too. Having to rely on technology to keep a grasp on it only makes it worse." He stepped down onto the sidewalk and backed away a few feet, arms crossed. "That bag of his stuff that I brought from the funeral home, most of it was clothes, his wallet and watch, all that. He would wear the shittiest cologne, always did. When we were younger it was because he didn't know any better, but once he found out it drove me nuts it was a point of pride for him. He'd get the worst shit too, some Benetton cologne he got on sale lasted him forever. It was godawful. I pulled the last shirt he ever wore out of that bag and it was just coated in it. Every morning for as long as it lasted I'd sit on the edge of my bed and smell that stupid shirt, crying some of the time…feeling guilty if I didn't. Breathed it in knowing it would fade a little more every day. Fade until it was nothing. You keep things that force you to remember; rituals you hang onto out of fear and out of respect. You keep going. Eventually something will change. Life isn't done with you yet."

We stood silently for a moment, both of us watching a car that passed by The Five slowly. Then another car pulled into the lot and parked at the farthest end away from the building. "If THIS ritual helps some people," Joe said, pointing his finger at the front door, "that's how food matters. That was your big question, right? What makes food matter?"

"Yeah Joe," I said, "and I think this answers a lot of it."

He stepped back up so that he was next to me. He smiled and nodded. "Everybody has their cute stories and theories, and that's fine. But for me, it's when things are so dark and so shitty that you can't process reality, you can barely breathe…when you are completely shut down…it's the only thing you can stomach to keep you from dying. The only thing. Even if you had your pick of everything from every restaurant in the world, all of it was available to you, and your body had to force you to pick that single thing…what was it then?"

The lights on the car in the parking lot went dark. The interior lights came on as the door opened. Joe touched my shoulder to take me back through the door.

"Come on in, you have to try some of this soup."

ABOUT THE AUTHOR

The Bad News Cafe is the first novel from author Hunter S.
Fatback. He is a native of Kansas City, and in addition to
writing for lifestyle magazines such as *Cigar and Spirits*, he
publishes local food and culture content on
www.huntersfatback.com. With a history of diverse
personal reinventions and life experiences, his strength lies
in his ability to sift through the fringes where the sacred
and profane overlap.